W9-BBE-875

THE MCCAFFERTYS: SLADE

This Large Print Book carries the Seal of Approval of N.A.V.H.

THE MCCAFFERTYS: SLADE

LISA JACKSON

WHEELER PUBLISHING
An imprint of Thomson Gale, a part of The Thomson Corporation

Detroit • New York • San Francisco • New Haven, Conn. • Waterville, Maine • London

5/07

THOMSON
★ ™
GALE

LP
Fic
JACKSON

LIBRARY OF CONGRESS CATALOGING-IN-PUBLICATION DATA

Jackson, Lisa.
   The McCaffertys — Slade / by Lisa Jackson.
     p. cm. — (The McCaffertys series ; #3) (Wheeler Publishing large print romance)
   ISBN-13: 978-1-59722-501-4 (alk. paper)
   ISBN-10: 1-59722-501-0 (alk. paper)
   1. Large type books. I. Title.
PS3560.A223M365 2007
813'.54—dc22   2006102842

Published in 2007 by arrangement with Harlequin Books S.A.

Printed in the United States of America on permanent paper
10 9 8 7 6 5 4 3 2 1

Dear Reader,

I think this is a fabulous idea! HQN is republishing one of my most popular series, THE McCAFFERTYS.

When the first book of the miniseries, *The McCaffertys: Thorne,* came out, I received a lot of letters and tons of e-mail asking questions about the McCafferty brothers and their wayward younger sister. With each new book in the series, I received more and more mail. The sexy, irreverent McCafferty brothers were extremely popular. And I can see why. I fell in love with each of these men who were tough, rugged and dedicated to their family and strong Montana ranching roots.

In each of the books one McCafferty brother discovers true love while trying to protect his younger sister and solve the mystery surrounding her baby. The series was finally complete with *Best-Kept Lies,*

Randi McCafferty's story. The mystery surrounding the paternity of Randi McCafferty's baby and the danger facing the McCafferty clan is wrapped up in the final book, where eventually Randi, too, discovers love everlasting for her and her son.

CEO Thorne McCafferty has returned to Grand Hope, Montana, and the Flying M Ranch, intent on taking charge of the situation with his sister. Once he's assured that Randi and her baby are healthy, he plans to cut and run, but that's before he meets beautiful Dr. Nicole Stevenson, a woman he knew as a girl but barely remembers. For the first time in his life Thorne's about to lose control. . . .

Rancher Matt McCafferty doesn't believe he could be interested in a professional woman of any kind, least of all a cop. But during the investigation of his sister's hit-and-run accident, he encounters a spitfire of a detective in Kelly Dillinger. Then his mind, his heart and his life change. . . .

Maverick Slade McCafferty never expected to run across Jamie Parsons again. The last time he saw her she was a young girl, one who had willingly given him her innocence. Now she's all grown up, a no-nonsense lawyer who won't give him the time of day. Or so she thinks.

Headstrong reporter Randi McCafferty doesn't want, need, or accept a bodyguard, but her brothers have hired Kurt Striker to watch her back. Kurt doesn't seem too thrilled with the job either, but as the danger mounts, the tension and unspoken passion ignite, just as a killer is ready to strike.

I've posted excerpts from the books on my Web site and I even have a new contest and drawing to celebrate THE McCAF-FERTYS. So visit me at www.lisajackson-.com and sign up. You just might win an autographed Lisa Jackson classic!

I hope you love the McCAFFERTYS as much as I do!

Lisa Jackson

PROLOGUE

There he was, sitting in his damned rocking chair as if it were a throne.

Slade McCafferty gnashed his back teeth and felt the taste of crow on his tongue as he glared through the bug-spattered windshield of his truck to the broad front porch of the ranch house he'd called home for the first twenty years of his life.

The old man, John Randall McCafferty, sat ramrod straight. In a way Slade respected him for his tenacious hold on life, his stubbornness, his determination to bend all of his children's wills to meet his own goals. The trouble was, it hadn't worked. The eldest McCafferty son, Thorne, was a hotshot attorney, a millionaire who ran his own corporation from Denver, and the second-born, Matt, had struck out on his own and bought himself a spread near the Idaho border. Randi, the youngest, Slade's half sister, lived in Seattle, and wrote her own syndicated column for a newspaper there.

That left Slade.

Ever the black sheep.

Ever the rogue.

Ever in trouble.

Not that he gave a damn.

As Slade eased out of the truck, a sharp pain shot through his hip and he winced, feeling the skin tighten around the barely visible scar that ran down one side of his face, a reminder of deeper marks that cut into his heart, the pain that never really left him. Well, no doubt he'd hear about that, too.

He paused to light a cigarette, then hobbled up the path through the sparse, dry grass that served as a lawn. Though it was barely May, it had been a dry spring, hotter than usual for this time of year, and the sun-bleached grass was testament to the unseasonable and arid weather.

John Randall didn't say a word, didn't so much as sway in the rocker as he watched his youngest son through narrowed eyes. A breeze, fiery as Satan's breath, scorched across the slight rise that supported the old ranch house. Two stories of weathered siding with dark-green trim around each window, the house had been a refuge once, then a battlefield, and later a prison. At least to Slade's way of thinking.

He sucked hard on his filter tip, felt the warmth of smoke curl through his lungs and faced the man who had sired him. "Dad." His boots rang as he hitched up the steps and John Randall's old hunting dog, Harold, lifted his graying head, then thumped his tail on the dusty planks. "Hi, boy."

More thumps.

"I thought you might not come."

"You said it was important." Jeez, the old man looked bad. Thin tufts of white hair barely covered his speckled pate, and his eyes, once a laser-blue, had faded. His hands were gnarled and his body frail, the wheelchair parked near the door evidence of his failing health, but there was still a bit of steel in John Randall's backbone, a measure of McCafferty grit in the set of his jaw.

"It is. Sit." He pointed toward a bench pushed under a window, but Slade leaned against the rail and faced him. The sun beat against his back.

"What's so all-fired important?"

"I want a grandson."

"What?" Slade's chest tightened and he felt the same old pain pound through his brain.

"You heard me. I don't have much time,

Slade, and I'd like to go to my grave knowin' that you've settled down, started a family, kept the family name alive."

"Maybe I'm not the one you should be talking to about this." Not now, not when the memories were so fresh.

"I've already had my say with Thorne and Matt. It's your turn."

"I'm not interested in —"

"I know about Rebecca." Slade braced himself. "And the baby."

Slade's head pounded as if a thousand horses were running through his brain. His scar seemed to pulse. "Yeah, well, it's something I've got to live with," he said, his eyes drilling into the old man's. "And it's hell."

"It wasn't your fault."

"So I've heard."

"You can't go beating yourself up one side and down the other the rest of your life," his father said with more compassion than Slade thought him capable of. "They're gone. It was a horrid accident. A painful loss. But life goes on."

"Does it?" Slade mocked, then wished he could call back the cruel words. He'd said them without thinking that his father was surely dying.

"Yes, it does. You can't stop living because

12

of a tragedy." He reached into the pocket of his vest and pulled out his watch, a silver-and-gold pocket watch engraved with the crest of the Flying M, this very ranch, his pride and joy. "I want you to have this."

"No, Dad. You keep it."

The old man's lips twisted into an ironic grin. "Don't have any use for it. Not where I'm goin'. But you do. I want you to keep it as a reminder of me." He pressed the timepiece into Slade's palm. "Don't waste your life, son. It's shorter than you think. Now, it's time for you to put the past behind you. Settle down. Start a family."

"I don't think so."

A fly buzzed near John Randall's head and he swatted at it with one gnarled hand. "Do me a favor, Slade. Quit moving long enough to figure out what you want in life. Whether you know it or not, what you need is a good woman. A wife. A mother for your children."

"You're a fine one to talk," Slade growled, dropping his cigarette to the floorboards where he crushed out the butt with his boot heel.

"I made my share of mistakes," his father admitted.

Slade didn't comment.

"I was young and foolish."

"Like I am now? Is that what you're trying to say?"

"No. I'm just hoping you'll learn from my mistakes."

"Mistakes. You mean, your two marriages? Or your two divorces?"

"Maybe both."

Slade glanced over his shoulder to the rolling hills of the ranch. Dust plumed behind a sorry old tractor chugging over one rise. "And you think I should get married."

"I believe in the institution."

"Even though it stripped you clean?"

John Randall sighed. "It wasn't so much the money that mattered," he said with more honesty than Slade expected. "But I betrayed a good woman and let you boys down. I lost the respect of my children, and that . . . that was hard to take. Don't get me wrong, if I had to do it again, I would. Remember if I hadn't taken up with Penelope, I would never have had my daughter."

"So it was worth it."

"Yes," he said, pushing the rocker so that it began to move a bit. "And I only hope that someday you'll forgive me, but more than that, Slade, I hope you find yourself a woman who'll make you believe in love again."

Slade pushed himself upright. "Don't

count on it." He dropped the watch into his father's lap.

CHAPTER ONE

Seven months later

The McCaffertys! Why in the world did her meeting have to be with the damned Mc-Cafferty brothers?

Jamie Parsons braked hard and yanked on the steering wheel as she reached the drive of her grandmother's small farm. Her wheezing compact turned too quickly. Tires spun in the snow that covered the two ruts where dry weeds had the audacity to poke through the blanket of white.

The cottage, in desperate need of repairs and paint, seemed quaint now, like some fairy-tale version of Grandma's house.

It had been, she thought as she grabbed her briefcase and overnight bag, then plowed through three inches of white powder to the back door. She found the extra key over the window ledge where her grandmother, Nita, had always kept it. "Just in

17

case, Jamie," she'd always explained in her raspy, old-lady voice. "We don't want to be locked out now, do we?"

No, Nana, we sure don't. Jamie's throat constricted when she thought of the woman who had taken in a wild, rebellious teenager; opened her house and her heart to a girl whose parents had given up on her. Nana hadn't batted an eye, just told her, from the time she stepped over the front threshold with her two suitcases, one-eyed teddy bear and an attitude that wouldn't quit, that things were going to change. From that moment forward, Jamie was to abide by her rules and that was that.

Not that they'd always gotten along.

Not that Jamie hadn't done everything imaginable behind the woman's broad back.

Not that Jamie hadn't tried every trick in the book to get herself thrown out of the only home she'd ever known.

Nana, a God-fearing woman who could cut her only granddaughter to the quick with just one glance, had never given up. Unlike everyone else in Jamie's life.

Now the key turned easily, and Jamie walked into the kitchen. It smelled musty, the black-and-white tiles covered in dust, the old Formica-topped table with chrome legs still pushed against the far wall that sloped sharply due to the stairs running up the other side of the house from the foyer. The salt and pepper shakers, in the shape of kittens, had disappeared from the table, as had all other signs of life. There were light spots in the wall, circular patches of clean paint where one of the antique dishes Nana had displayed with pride had been taken down and given to some relative somewhere in accordance with Nita's will. A dried cactus in a plastic pot had been forgotten and pushed into a corner of the counter where once there had been a toaster. The gingham curtains were now home to spiders whose webs gathered more dust.

If Nana had been alive, she would have had a fit. This kitchen had always gleamed. "Cleanliness is next to godliness," she'd preached while pushing a broom, or polishing a lamp, or scrubbing a sink. And Nana had known about godliness; she'd read her Bible every evening, never missed a Sunday sermon and taught Sunday school to teenagers.

God, Jamie missed her.

The bulk of Nana's estate, which consisted of this old house, the twenty acres surrounding it and a 1940 Chevrolet parked in the old garage, had been left to Jamie. It was Nana's dream that Jamie settle down here in Grand Hope, live in the little cottage, get married and have half a dozen great-grandchildren for her to spoil. "Sorry," Jamie said out loud as she dropped her bags on the table and ran a finger through the fine layer of dust that had collected on the chipped Formica top. "I just never got around to it."

She glanced at the sink where she envisioned her short, round grandmother with her gray permed hair, thick waist and heavy arms. Nita Parsons would have been wearing her favorite tattered apron. In the summertime she would have been putting up peaches and pears or making strawberry jam. This time of year she would have been baking dozens upon dozens of tiny Christmas cookies that she meticulously iced and decorated before giving boxes of the delicacies to friends and relatives. Nana's old yellow-and-white spotted cat, Lazarus, would have been doing figure eights and rubbing up against Nita's swollen ankles, and she would have complained now and again about the arthritis that had invaded her fingers and shoulders.

"Oh, Nana," Jamie whispered, glancing out the window to the snow-crusted yard. Thorny, leafless brambles scaled the wire fence surrounding the garden plot. The henhouse had nearly collapsed. The small barn was still standing, though the roof sagged and the remaining weed-strewn pasture was thankfully hidden beneath the blanket of white.

Nana had loved it here, and Jamie intended to clean it up and list it with a local real estate company.

She glanced at her watch and walked outside to the back porch. She couldn't waste any more time thinking maudlin, nostalgic thoughts. She had too much to do, including meeting with the McCafferty brothers.

Boy, and won't that be a blast? She carried in her bags and, despite the near-zero weather, opened every window on the first floor to air out the house. Then she climbed up the steep wooden stairs to her bedroom tucked under the eaves. It was as she'd left it years ago, with the same hand-pieced quilt tossed over the spindle bed. She opened the shades and window and looked past the naked branches of an oak tree to the county road that passed this stretch of farmland. All in all, the area hadn't changed much. Though the town of Grand Hope had grown, Nana had lived far enough outside the city limits that the fast lane hadn't quite reached her.

Jamie unpacked. She hung some clothes in the old closet, the rest she stowed in the top two drawers of an antique bureau. She didn't allow her mind to drift back to the year and a half she'd lived with Nana, the best time of her life . . . and the worst. For the first time in her seventeen years she'd understood the meaning of unconditional love, given her by an elderly woman with sparkling gold eyes, rimless glasses and a wisdom that spanned nearly seven decades. Yet Jamie had also experienced her first love and heartbreak compliments of Slade-the-bastard-McCafferty.

And whoop-de-do, she probably was going to meet him again this very afternoon. Life was just chock-full of surprises. And sometimes they weren't for the best.

It took two hours to check in the barn and find that Caesar, Nana's old gelding, was waiting for her. A roan with an ever-graying nose, Caesar was more than twenty years old, but his eyes were bright and clear, and from the shine on his winter coat, Jamie knew that the neighbors had been taking care of him.

"Bet you still get lonely, though, eh, boy?" she asked, seeing to his water and feed and taking in the smell of him and the small, dusty barn. He nickered softly, and Jamie's eyes burned with unshed tears. How could she ever sell him? "We had some good times together, you and I, didn't we? Got into our share of trouble."

She cleared her throat and found a brush to run over his shoulders and back as memories of racing him across the wide expanse of Montana grassland flashed through her eyes. She even rode him to the river where he waded into the deeper water and swam across, all at the urging of Slade McCafferty. Jamie had never forgotten the moment of exhilaration as Caesar had floated with the current. Slade's blue eyes had danced, and he'd showed her a private deer trail where they'd stopped and smoked forbidden cigarettes.

Her heart twisted at the memory. "Yep, you're quite a trooper," she told the horse. "I'll be back. Soon." Hurrying into the house, determined to leave any memory of Slade behind her, she worked for the next two hours getting the ancient old furnace running, turning on the water, adjusting the temperature of the water heater, then stripping her bed only to make it again with sheets that had been packed away in a cedar chest. She smiled sadly as she stretched the soft percale over the mattress. It smelled slightly of lavender — Nana's favorite scent.

Again her heart ached. God, she missed her grandmother, the one person in the world she could count on. Rather than tackle any serious cleaning, she set up a makeshift office in the dining room compliments of her laptop computer and a modem; she only had to call the phone company and set up service again; then, she could link to the office in Missoula.

She checked her watch. She had less than an hour before she was to sit down with Thorne, Matt and Slade McCafferty. The Flying M ranch was nearly twenty miles away.

"Better get a move on, Parsons," she told herself though her stomach was already clenched in tight little knots at the thought of coming face-to-face with Slade again. It was ridiculous, really. How could something that happened so long ago still bother her?

She'd been over Slade McCafferty for years. *Years.*

Seeing him again would be no problem at all, just another day in a lawyer's life, the proverbial walk in the park. Right? So why, then, the tightness in her chest, the acceleration of her heartbeat, the tiny beads of sweat gathering under her scalp on this cold day? For crying out loud, she was acting like an adolescent, and that just wouldn't do. Not at all.

Back up the stairs.

She changed from jeans and her favorite old sweater to a black suit with a silk blouse and knee-high boots, then wound her hair into a knot she pinned to the top of her head, and gazed at her reflection in the mirror above the antique dresser. It had been nearly fifteen years since she'd seen Slade McCafferty, and in those years she'd blossomed from a fresh-faced, angry eighteen-year-old with something to prove to a full-grown adult who'd worked two jobs to get through college and eventually earned a law degree.

The woman in the reflection was confident, steady and determined, but beneath the image, Jamie saw herself as she had been: heavier, angrier, the new-girl-in-town with a bad attitude and even worse reputation.

A nest of butterflies erupted in her stomach at the thought of dealing with Slade again, but she told herself she was being silly, reliving those melodramatic teenage years. Which was just plain nuts! Angry with herself, she pulled on black gloves and a matching wool coat, grabbed her briefcase and purse, and was down the stairs and out

Nana's back door in nothing flat. She trudged through the snow to her little car, carrying her briefcase as if it were some kind of shield. Lord, she was a basket case. So she had to face Slade McCafferty again.

So what?

So far, it had been a bad day.

And it was only going to get worse.

Slade could feel it in his bones.

He leaned a shoulder against the window casing and stared out the dining room window to the vast, snow-covered acres of the Flying M ranch and the surrounding forested hills. Cattle moved sluggishly across the wintry landscape, and gray clouds threatened to drop more snow on this section of the valley. The temperature was hovering just below freezing, and his hip ached a little, a reminder that he hadn't quite healed from last year's skiing accident.

Thorne was seated at the long table where the family gathered for holidays and special occasions. He'd shoved the holly and mistletoe centerpiece to one side and had spread out documents in neat piles. He was still wearing a leg brace from a plane crash that had nearly taken his life, and he propped that leg on a nearby chair as he sorted through the papers.

Damn, he was such a control freak.

"You're sure you want to sell?" he asked for the dozenth time.

They'd been over this time and time again.

Slade didn't bother answering.

"Where will you go?"

"Not sure." He shrugged. Craved a smoke. "I'll hang around for a while. Long enough to nail the bastard who messed up Randi."

White lines bracketed Thorne's mouth. "I can't wait for the day." He shoved his chair back. "It won't come soon enough for me."

"Me, either."

"You heard anything from Striker?" Thorne asked, bringing up the P.I. whom Slade had brought into the investigation.

"Nope. Left a message this morning."

"You sure about him?" Thorne asked.

"I'd trust my life with him."

"You're trusting Randi's."

"Give it a rest, will ya?" Slade snapped. Everyone's nerves were stretched to the breaking point. Slade had known Kurt Striker for years and had brought him in to investigate the attempts on their half sister Randi's life. Kelly Dillinger, Matt's fiancée, had joined up with Striker. She'd once been with the sheriff's department; she was now working the private side.

"You doubt Kurt Striker's ability?"

Thorne shook his hand. "Nah. Just frustrated. I want this over."

"You and me both."

Slade would like to move on. He'd been restless here at the Flying M, never did feel that this old ranch house was home, not since his parents' divorce some twenty-odd years earlier. But he'd planned to stay in Grand Hope, Montana, until the person who was terrorizing his half sister and her newborn baby was run to ground and locked away forever. Or put six feet under. He didn't really care which.

He just needed to find a new life. Whatever the hell it was. Ever since Rebecca . . . No, he wouldn't go there. Couldn't. It was still too damned painful.

Now, it's time for you to put the past behind you. Settle down. Start a family. His father's advice crept up on him like a ghost.

Bootsteps rang in the hallway.

"Sorry I'm late —" Matt apologized as he strode in. Propped against his shoulder was J.R., Randi's baby, now nearly two months old. The kid had captured each one of his uncles' jaded hearts, something the women around this neck of the woods had thought impossible.

Matt adjusted the baby on his shoulder, and J.R. made a strange gurgling sound that pulled at the corners of Slade's mouth. With downy, uneven reddish-blond hair that stuck up at odd angles no matter how often Randi smoothed it, big eyes that took in everything, and a button of a nose, J.R. acted as if he owned the place. He flailed his tiny fists and often sucked on not only his thumb, but whatever digit was handy. "I was busy changing this guy."

Thorne chuckled. "*That's* your excuse for being late?"

"It's my *reason.*"

Slade swallowed a smile, his mood improving. The little one; he was a reason to stick around here awhile.

"Okay, so let's get down to business," Thorne suggested. "Aside from the papers about the land sale, I'm going to ask about checking into the baby's father, seeing what his rights are."

"Randi won't like it," Matt predicted.

"Of course she won't. She doesn't like much of anything these days."

Amen, Slade thought, but he didn't blame his sister for being restless and feeling cooped up. He'd experienced the same twinges. It was time to move on . . . as soon as the bastard who was terrorizing her was put away.

Thorne added, "I'm only doing what's

best for her."

"That'll make her like it less." Slade rested a hip on the edge of the table.

"Too bad. When Ms. Parsons arrives, I'm going to bring it up."

Ms. Jamie Parsons, Attorney-at-Law.

Slade's back teeth ground together at the thought of her. He'd never expected to see her again; hadn't wanted to. Still didn't. He'd dated her for a while, true, and there had been something about her that had left him wanting more, but he'd dated a lot of women in his lifetime, before and after Jamie Parsons. It wasn't a big deal.

"Why do I think you've been discussing me?" Randi asked as she appeared in the doorway to the dining room. She was limping slightly from the accident that had nearly taken her life, but her spine was stiff as she hobbled into the room and pried the baby easily from Matt's arms.

"You always think we're talkin' about you behind your back," Matt teased.

"Because you always are. Right?" she asked Slade.

"Always," he drawled.

"So when's the attorney due to arrive?"

Thorne checked his watch. "In about fifteen minutes."

"Good." Randi kissed her son's head and

he cooed softly. Slade felt a pang deep inside, a pain he buried deep. He touched the scar on the side of his face and scowled. He wasn't envious of Randi — God, no. But he couldn't help being reminded of his own loss every time he looked at his nephew.

And his sister had been through so much. Aside from the fact that she still moved with difficulty, wincing once in a while from the pain, there was the problem with her memory. Amnesia, if she could be believed.

Slade wasn't convinced. Nope. He wasn't certain his half sister was being straight with them. Her memory loss smacked of convenience. There were just too many questions Randi didn't want to answer, questions concerning her son's paternity. When her jaw had been wired shut and her arm in a cast, communication had been near impossible, but now she was well on the way to being a hundred percent again. Except for her mind. To Slade's way of thinking, amnesia made everything so much easier. No explanations. Not even about the damned accident that had nearly ended her life.

What the hell had happened on that icy road in Glacier Park? All Slade, his brothers and the police knew was that Randi's Jeep had swerved off the road and down an

31

embankment. Had she hit ice? Been forced off the road? Kurt Striker, the private investigator Slade had contacted to look into the accident, was convinced another car, a maroon Ford product, had forced Randi off the road. The police were checking. Only Randi knew for certain. And she wasn't talking.

The result of the accident had been premature delivery of the baby, internal injuries, concussion, lacerations, a broken jaw and a fractured leg. She'd spent most of her recuperation time in a coma, unable to communicate, while the brothers had searched for whoever had tried to harm her and her baby.

So far, they'd come up empty. Whoever had tried to kill Randi had taken a second shot at it, slipping into the hospital, posing as part of the staff and injecting insulin into her IV. She'd survived. Barely. And the maniac was still very much at large.

Slade's fists clenched at the thought of the bastard. If he ever got his hands on the guy, he'd beat the living tar out of him.

But Randi wasn't helping much. She'd emerged from her coma fighting mad and unwilling to help. If only she'd help them, give them some names, let them know who might want to harm her. . . . But no. Her memory just kept failing her.

Or so she claimed.

Bull.

Slade figured she was hiding something, covering up the truth, protecting someone. But why? Who?

Herself? Her baby? Little J.R.'s father, whoever he was? Or someone else?

"Hell," he growled under his breath.

Maybe Thorne was right. Maybe they should enlist Jamie Parsons and the firm of Jansen, Monteith and Stone to try to locate the baby's father and to take the legal steps to ensure that J.R.'s daddy wouldn't show up someday and demand custody. If that was even possible.

Slade just wished the lawyer assigned to their case was someone other than Jamie Parsons.

Randi settled into the chair directly across the table from Thorne. "Since the attorney's dropping by anyway, I want to talk about changing the baby's name legally. J.R. doesn't cut it with me."

"Do what you want. We needed something for the birth certificate." Thorne glanced at his nephew. "But I think J.R. fits him just fine."

"So do I," Slade agreed. "Since you were in a coma, we agreed on the initials."

"Okay, okay, so it served a purpose and now everyone is calling him J.R., but I'm going to change his name officially to Joshua Ray McCafferty." She glanced around the room, and if she saw the questions in her brothers' eyes, ignored them.

J.R.'s paternity was a touchy subject. With everyone. Particularly Randi, who was the only one who could name the father. But she wasn't talking. Unmarried and, to her brothers' knowledge, not seriously involved with anyone, she refused to name the man.

Why?

"He's mine," she'd say when asked about the baby. "That's all that matters."

But it bothered Slade. A lot. He couldn't help but think her reticence to name the man and the attempts on her life were related.

"He's your kid. You can name him whatever you want," Thorne said agreeably, "but I didn't warn the attorney that we'd have more issues than the property division."

"He'll handle it." Randi adjusted the drool bib around her son's tiny neck.

"She," Thorne clarified. "Chuck Jansen is sending a woman associate. Jamie Parsons. She grew up around here."

"Jamie?" Randi's eyes narrowed thoughtfully and Slade envisioned the gears in her mind meshing and spinning and spewing out all kinds of unwanted conclusions. Yep. She glanced his way.

"She lived with her grandmother outside of town." Thorne winced as he adjusted his bad leg on the chair next to him.

"Nita Parsons. Yes, I remember. Mom made me take piano lessons from Mrs. Parsons. Man, she was a taskmaster."

None of the men commented. They never liked to be reminded that Randi's mother had been the reason their parents had divorced. John Randall had fallen in love with Penelope Henley, promptly divorced Larissa, their mother, and married the much younger woman. Six months after the nuptials, Randi had come into the world. Slade hadn't much liked his stepmother or the new baby, but over the years he'd quit blaming his half sister for his parents' doomed union.

Randi looked up at Slade and he felt it coming — the question he didn't want to face. "Weren't you and Jamie an item years ago?"

"Hardly an item. We saw each other a few times. It wasn't a big deal." He shoved his hands into the back pockets of his jeans and hoped that was the end of it. But he knew his reporter sister better than that.

"More than a few. And, if I remember right, she was pretty gone on you."

"Is that right?" Matt asked, a smile crawling across his beard-shadowed chin. "Hard to believe any woman would be so foolish."

"Isn't it?" Randi said as J.R. tried to grab her earring.

"Funny. I wouldn't think you'd *remember* anything."

Randi's eyes flashed. "Bits and pieces, Slade. I already told you, I just remember a little of this and a little of that. More each day."

But not the father of her child? Or what happened when she was forced off the road?

"Then you'd better focus on who wants to see you dead."

"You were involved with the lady lawyer?" Matt asked.

Slade lifted one shoulder and felt the weight of his brothers' gazes on him. "It was a long time ago." He heard the whine of an engine and his muscles tightened. He turned toward the window.

Through the frosty panes he caught a glimpse of a tiny blue car chugging its way along the drive. Slade's gut clenched. The compact slid to a stop, narrowly missing his truck. A couple of seconds later a tall woman emerged from the car. With a black

36

briefcase swinging from her arm, she hesitated just a second as she looked at the house, then taking a deep breath, she squared her shoulders and strode up the front path where the snow had been broken and trampled.

Jamie Parsons in the flesh.

Great. Just . . . great.

She was all confidence and femininity in her severe black coat. Sunstreaked hair had been slicked away from a face that boasted high cheekbones, defined chin, and wide forehead. He couldn't make out the color of her eyes but remembered they were hazel, shifting from green to gold in the sunlight or darkening when she got angry.

For a second he flashed upon a time when the two of them had been down by the creek, not far from the swimming hole where Thorne had almost drowned.

It had been a torridly hot summer, the wildflowers had been in bloom, the grass dry and the smell of fresh-cut hay had floated in the air along with the fluff from dandelions. He'd dared her to strip naked and jump into the clear water. And she, with the look of devilment in those incredible eyes, had done just that, exposing high, firm breasts with pink nipples and a thatch of reddish hair above long, tanned legs. He'd caught only a glimpse before she'd dashed into the water, submerged and come up tossing her wet hair from her eyes. He could still hear her laughter, melodious as a warbler's song.

God, where had that come from? It had been eons ago. A lifetime. The bad day just got worse.

From somewhere on the front porch Harold gave up a deep "woof" just as the doorbell chimed.

"You gonna get that?" Matt asked, and Slade, frowning, headed along the hallway toward the front door.

From the kitchen Juanita, the housekeeper, was rattling pans and singing softly in Spanish, while in the living room a fire crackled and Nicole, Thorne's wife, was playing a board game with her four-year-old twin daughters. Giggles and quiet conversation could be heard over the muted melodies of Christmas carols playing from a recently purchased CD player. At the sound of the front door chimes, two little voices erupted.

"I get it! I get it!"

"No. Me!"

Two sets of small feet scurried through the living room as Molly and Mindy, their dark ringlets flying, scrambled into the entry hall and raced for the door. Small hands vying for the handle, they managed to yank the door open and there on the front porch, looking professional, feminine and surprised as all get-out at her reception, stood Jamie Parsons, Attorney-at-Law.

CHAPTER TWO

"Who're *you?*" Molly demanded, her brown eyes trained on the woman in black.

"I'm Jamie." With one quick glance at Slade, she bent down on one knee, mindless that her coat was getting wet in the snow melting on the floorboards of the porch. Good Lord, he'd gotten better looking! "And who are you?" she asked one girl.

"Molly," the bolder twin asserted, rubbing a hand on her pink sweatshirt.

"And you?" Jamie's eyes moved to Molly's identical sister. They were Slade's daughters, she thought wildly. Surprised that she cared. "What's your name?"

Mindy took a step behind Slade's jeans-clad leg. Her small arms wrapped around his knee and she hid her face.

"She's Mindy and she's shy," Molly stated.

"Am not." Mindy's thumb was suddenly in her mouth as she peeked around Slade's thigh. Slade was amused as he read Jamie's case of nerves. Another set of footsteps announced Nicole's arrival. Tall, slender, with amber eyes and blond-streaked hair, she was a doctor at St. James Hospital and the mother of the imps, not to mention the reason Thorne wore a smile these days.

"Hello," she said to Jamie. "I'm Nicole McCafferty." She extended a hand and tossed a lock of hair off her shoulder. "And these two tornados —" she indicated the twins with her chin "— are my daughters."

Straightening, Jamie accepted Nicole's handshake. She glanced at Slade, and something dark shifted in her hazel eyes. Her smile became a little more forced, her voice more professional and cool. "Pleased to meet you. All of you."

"I take it you already know Slade?" Nicole said as she peeled Mindy from Slade's leg and gathered the shy girl into her arms.

"Yes . . . we've . . . we've met. Years ago." Jamie's voice was husky and she cleared her throat.

Slade noticed that she inched her chin up a fraction as she turned to him and, gesturing to the girls, said, "You've been busy."

He lifted one eyebrow.

"Your daughters . . . they're lovely," she added.

"Why thank you," he drawled, smothering

41

a smile at her discomfiture — now what was that all about? "But they're not mine."

"Oh. I'm sorry. I was married before," Nicole explained. "I just recently joined this family."

"I see."

Nicole laughed as she finally caught on. "Oh. No. *No!* It's not what you think. Slade's my brother-in-law. I'm married to Thorne."

"Poor woman," Slade drawled, and Nicole sent him a dirty look. He witnessed a blush steal up Jamie's neck. He remembered that. How easily her fair skin would color a soft, embarrassed pink.

"Oh. Well. My mistake." Was she relieved? "There wasn't any reference to wives in the documents."

"*That* will have to be changed." Nicole chuckled and stepped out of the doorway as a black-and-white-spotted cat darted up the stairs. "Come in. It's freezing out there. Let me take your coat, and Slade — if he has a gentlemanly bone in his body, which is highly unlikely in my opinion — can show you into the dining room where the rest of the clan is waiting."

"I can manage that," Slade allowed.

"I hope so." Nicole transferred a squirming Mindy to the floor. "Meanwhile, I'll see if Juanita can scrounge up some coffee or tea."

Jamie was working the buttons of her coat. "That would be great."

"I'll take that," Slade offered as Nicole headed toward the kitchen, her daughters trailing after her like ducklings behind a mother duck.

Jamie set her bags down and shrugged out of her overcoat with Slade's help. His fingers brushed her nape for the briefest of seconds and he thought she stiffened, but he might have imagined it. She probably barely remembered him.

All business in a black suit and shimmery blouse, she picked up her bags again. "Ready?" she asked.

"As I'll ever be." He showed her along the hallway to the dining room. They passed by what he referred to as the McCafferty Hall of Shame where photos of the family were mounted. With cool disinterest Jamie's eyes skimmed pictures of Thorne in his football uniform, Randi going to the prom, Matt on a bucking bronco and Slade skiing downhill as if the devil were on his tail. Jamie didn't react, just walked smartly into the dining room.

"Hi," she said. "You all probably know this, but I figured I'd better get the formal introductions over. I'm Jamie Parsons with Jansen, Monteith and Stone." Thorne had some trouble scrambling to his feet as one of his legs was in a brace, but Matt reached forward to shake her hand. Slade made quick introductions. "All right," she said, offering them each a smile that Slade was certain she'd practiced a thousand times in front of a mirror, "let's get started."

Everyone settled into a chair. Jamie flipped open her briefcase and distributed copies of legal documents. "The way I understand it is that Matt —" she pinned the middle Mc-Cafferty brother in her gaze "— wants to sell his place north of Missoula on contract to Michael Kavanaugh, his neighbor. He then wants to buy the two of you —" she motioned to Slade and Thorne "— out, so that he'll own half of this place and, Randi, you'll own the other half."

"That's right," Matt confirmed.

"Matt's agreed to run the ranch," Randi contributed. "Then he . . . well, he and Kelly, since they're going to be married soon . . . can live here."

"What about you?" Thorne asked, his brows beetling.

Randi shook her head and flipped a palm toward the ceiling. "I do have a life in Seattle, you know."

Thorne's scowl deepened. "Yeah, I do know. But until we're certain you're safe, I don't want you going anywhere. Not until we figure out who's been trying to kill you and he's safely behind bars."

With a smile that dared her oldest brother to try to tell her what to do, she arched a dark brow. "I'm not arguing about it now, okay? I think Ms. Parsons has business here and she'd like to get down to it."

"Jamie. Let's keep this casual."

Slade stiffened.

"We're all from around here, so there's no reason to be formal," Jamie said coolly. "Okay, you've all got a copy of the paperwork, so let's go over it."

Slade tried not to notice the slope of her jaw, or the way she flashed a smile or how her eyebrows knitted in concentration as she read through the documents. What had happened between them was ancient history. *Ancient.*

Besides, he didn't like lawyers. Any of 'em. He reached into his shirt pocket, his fingers searching for a nonexistent pack of cigarettes. He was trying to cut down and had left his smokes in his truck. Not that anyone would let him light up in here anyway.

Nicole brought in a tray of coffee, tea and cinnamon cookies, but Jamie seemed to barely notice. The baby started to fuss and she glanced at J.R. for just a second, her eyes turning wistful for the barest of moments before she became all business again.

Apologizing in Spanish and English, Juanita bustled in. Dark eyes flashed with pride as she fixated on the baby. "*Dios,* little man, you are a loud one." Expertly she plucked the infant from Randi's arms. "He is hungry, *sí?*"

"Big time," Randi said, starting to climb to her feet.

"Sit, sit . . . you have business." Juanita waved Randi back into her chair. "I'll see to him." Before Randi could protest, Juanita turned on her heel and, cradling the baby close, swept out of the room.

Jamie barely broke stride. "Let's look at page two . . ."

A professional attorney through and through, Slade thought, staring at her. Where was the wild, rebellious girl he remembered? The one who had turned his head and made him, for a few weeks, question what he wanted? The girl in tattered jeans who had, behind her grandmother's back, drunk, smoked and gone to a tattoo parlor, only to be kicked out before the deed was done as she was underage? If Slade's recollection was right, Jamie had planned to have a small butterfly etched into one smooth shoulder.

Glancing at the thick sheaf of neatly typed pages in front of him Slade wondered if Jamie, once she'd finally turned eighteen, had ever gone back for the body art? Or had her transformation into this all-business woman already begun? Who was she these days? Just another corporate attorney with her hair pulled harshly away from her face, her nails polished, her smile forced? Where was the free spirit who had attracted him so many years ago? Where was the rebellious creature who could spit as well as any boy, swear a blue streak, and ride bareback under the stars without a second's hesitation? He watched her through eyes at half mast and hardly caught a glimmer of the girl she'd once been. For today, at least, she was all business — an automaton spewing legal jargon.

Every once in a while one of the brothers or Randi asked a question. Jamie always had an answer.

"I'll want to put my fiancée's name on the deed," Matt said, his dark eyes thoughtful.

"So you're getting married." Jamie scribbled a quick note on her copy of the documents. "When?"

"Between Christmas and New Year's. I

47

tried to talk her into eloping, but her family had a fit. As it is, it's pretty short notice."

Jamie lifted an arched brow. "So another McCafferty bachelor bites the dust."

"Ouch," Thorne said, but one side of his mouth curved upward. "That just leaves Slade."

For a second the Ice Woman seemed to melt. Her hazel eyes found his. A dozen questions lurked therein. "I thought you were married."

"Never," he replied. Seated low on his spine, sipping coffee, he stared straight into those incredible eyes.

"But . . . I mean . . ." She seemed confused, then quickly shoved whatever she was thinking out of her mind and pulled her corporate self together. "Not that it matters. So . . ." She swung her head toward Matt who was seated at the head of the table near the china closet. "What's your fiancée's name?"

"Kelly Dillinger, but it will be McCafferty by the end of the month."

"She's the daughter of Eva Dillinger, who was our father's secretary." Thorne's mouth turned down and Slade's stomach twisted at the thought of his old man. He missed him, true, but the guy had been a number-one bastard most of Slade's life. "The deal

48

is this. Dad reneged on paying Eva the retirement that he'd promised her and so we —" he motioned to include his brothers and sister "— through the trust, decided to make it good. Your firm handles the disbursements."

Jamie gave a quick nod as if she suddenly remembered. "I've got the papers on the trust with me," she said, riffling through her briefcase and withdrawing another thick file.

"Good." Thorne nodded.

"But Kelly's name needs to be on the deed to the ranch," Matt insisted.

"Duly noted." Jamie penned a reminder on the first page of the contract allowing Matt to buy out his brothers. "I'll see that she's included in the final draft, then she'll have to sign, along with the rest of you, and Mr. Kavanaugh. I'll leave you each a copy of what I've drawn up and you can peruse everything more closely. If you all agree, I'll print out final copies and we'll sign."

"Sounds good." Matt picked up his set of papers as Jamie straightened her pile and thumped it on the table. With a well-practiced smile that didn't light her eyes, she glanced at each McCafferty sibling before sliding all the documents into her briefcase.

So rehearsed, so professional, so un-Jamie

Parsons. At least the Jamie he remembered. As he observed her, Slade wondered what it would take to catch a glimpse of the girl hiding beneath the neatly pressed jacket and skirt.

"So . . . Matt, you and your wife will be living on the property . . . Thorne and Nicole are building nearby and Randi will eventually move back to Seattle. I've got all your addresses except Slade's." She stared straight at him. "Where do you call home these days?"

"I've got a place in Colorado, outside of Boulder, but . . . I haven't decided if I'll stay there or sell it. In the meantime, I'm here, so you can use the address of the Flying M."

"Fair enough." She glanced again from one McCafferty sibling to the next. "Anything else?" she asked.

"Yeah." Thorne glanced at his sister. "We've got a little situation and I'd like some advice on it. As you know, Randi, here, had a baby a couple of months back and the father hasn't stepped forward and made any claim of custody yet, but —"

"Hey!" Randi shot out of her chair and skewered her brother with a don't-even-go-there glare. "Let's not get into this. Not now."

"We have to, Randi." Thorne was serious. "Sooner or later J.R.'s dad is gonna show up. I'll bet on it. And he's gonna start talking about custody and his rights as a father and I'd like to know what we're up against."

"This is *my* problem, Thorne," Randi said, leaning over the table. Pushing her face as close to her oldest brother's as was possible, she hooked a thumb at her chest. "Mine. Okay? Not yours. Not Matt's. Not Slade's. And certainly not Jansen, Monteith and Stone's!" Her eyes snapped fire, her cheeks flushed and she glared at Thorne for a long moment. No one said a word. Finally, Randi swung her gaze toward Jamie. "No offense, okay, but I can handle this. My brothers are just mad because I haven't told them who the baby's father is. Not that it's *any* of their business."

"There's a reason for that," Slade reminded her. "Someone's trying to kill you."

"Again, it's nobody's business."

"Like hell." Slade glowered at his sister. Sometimes Randi could be so bullheaded she was just plain stupid. "Your safety is our business."

"I can take care of myself."

"You can't even remember what happened!" Slade countered, disgusted with his half sibling. "At least that's what you claim."

"It's true."

"Okay, fine, then help us out. We're just trying to keep you safe. To keep J.R., or whatever the hell you call him, safe, okay? So quit being so damned bristly and give us a clue or two! Who's the kid's dad?"

"This isn't the time or place," she warned, every muscle tightening.

Thorne held up a hand as if to somehow quiet Slade. "We're just trying to help."

"Back off, Thorne. I said I can handle it. He's my baby and I would never, *never* do anything to put him in jeopardy, for God's sake. Now, I agreed to stay here for a while, until this whole mess is cleared up, but that doesn't mean my life is going to stop, so just back off!"

Matt shook his head and stared out the window.

"Women," Slade growled, and Jamie's spine stiffened.

Instead of snapping back at his remark, she visibly shifted, as if deciding it was her job to diffuse the argument rather than aggravate it. "Custody rights aren't my area of expertise, but, if you decide you do want some legal advice, I can hook you up with Felicia Reynolds. She handles all the custody cases for the firm."

"Thanks. Maybe *I'll* contact her." Randi

52

shot Thorne another warning glare before dropping into her chair. "Maybe."

Jamie snapped her briefcase closed. "Let me know if you want to get in touch with her."

"I will," Randi said, firing Thorne a look meant to not only kill but to eviscerate, as well.

"Okay." It was Jamie's turn to stand. "If any of you has any questions, you can call me through my cell phone, as I don't have a phone number here in town yet, or you can leave a message with the office and they'll get in touch with me. I'm staying at my grandmother's place and as soon as the regular phone is hooked up, I'll let you know."

The meeting was over.

Everyone shook hands.

All business.

Somehow it galled the hell out of Slade, but he found her coat and helped her into it.

Without a backward glance, she walked out the door, her black coat billowing behind her, her briefcase swinging from one gloved hand. Slade hesitated, couldn't help but watch as she climbed into her car and drove away, tires spinning in the snow.

"Randi's right. You did date her," Matt

said as Slade closed the door and, hands in the front pockets of his jeans, strolled back to the living room where his brothers were waiting. Matt knelt at the fire, prodding the blackened log with a poker while Thorne rummaged in the old man's liquor cabinet.

"I saw her a few times," Slade admitted, leaning one hip on the windowsill. This conversation was getting them nowhere and he didn't want to discuss it. Seeing Jamie again had brought back a tidal wave of memories that he'd dammed up a long, long time ago.

"Oh, come on, Slade. You saw her more than a few times." Randi hobbled into the room, then fell onto the leather couch. "Let's see," she said, her features pinching as she tried to recall images from the past. Slade sensed he wasn't going to like what was coming next and he braced himself. "The way I remember it, you dated Jamie for a couple of months while you were broken up with Sue Ellen Tisdale, right?"

"I remember you with Sue Ellen," Thorne added.

Great. Just what he needed: his family dissecting his love life.

"But," Randi added, "once Sue Ellen came to her senses and came running back, you dropped Jamie like a hot potato. I thought you were going to marry Sue El-len."

Slade snorted; didn't comment.

Thorne pulled out a bottle of Scotch. "So did I."

"Everyone did." Randi wasn't about to let up. "Probably even Jamie."

"Again, your memory amazes me," Slade commented.

"As I said, 'bits and pieces.' "

"Is that right?" Matt prodded the fire with a poker. "You really tossed Jamie over for Sue Ellen Tisdale?" His tone implied that Slade was a first-class idiot.

"That's not exactly what happened. Besides, it was years ago."

"Doesn't matter when it happened." Randi rested one heel on the coffee table. "Face it, Slade," she said as the fire began to crackle, "whether you want to admit it or not, about fifteen years ago, you were the son of a bitch who broke Jamie Parsons's heart."

CHAPTER THREE

"Well, that went swimmingly," Jamie rumbled under her breath as she carried her briefcase and a sack of groceries into her grandmother's house. Driving into town from the Flying M she'd second-guessed herself and cursed C. William "Chuck" Jansen a dozen times over for assigning her to the McCafferty project.

"Since you're heading to Grand Hope anyway, I thought you could help the firm out," Chuck had said as he'd sat familiarly on the corner of the desk in her office, one leg swinging, his wing-tip gleaming in the soft lighting. His boyish smile had been wide, his suit expensive, his shirt, as always, starched and crisply pressed. He'd tugged at his Yves St. Laurent tie. "I think it would be a good idea to put a face on Jansen, Monteith and Stone for the McCafferty family. John Randall McCafferty was an excellent client of the firm and the partners would like to keep the McCaffertys' business. Maybe even get a little more. Thorne McCafferty is a millionaire several times over in his own right, and the second son, Matt — he owns his own place. He's basically a small-time rancher, but he also seems to have some of that McCafferty-Midas touch. The third son . . ."

Jamie recalled how Chuck's brows had knit and his lips had folded together thoughtfully while she had conjured up a few unwelcome memories of Slade and nearly snapped her pen in two. "Well, there's always one in the family, I suppose. The third son, Slade — he never amounted to much. Lots of potential, but couldn't get it together. Too busy raising hell. He drove race cars and rode rodeo and even led expeditions for extreme skiing, I think. Always on the edge, but never getting his life together.

"But John Randall's only daughter, Randi — she's a real firecracker — takes after the old man. No wonder she was named after him."

Jamie tried to ignore the comments about Slade and concentrated on his half sister. She remembered Randi as being smart, sassy and McCafferty-stubborn.

"She's got her own daily column, 'Solo'

or 'Being Single' or something," Chuck had continued. "Writes for a Seattle newspaper. There's some talk of syndication, I think. And Thorne mentioned that she could have been working on a book at the time of the accident."

"Thorne McCafferty used to work here, didn't he?" Jamie had asked, twiddling her pen and not liking the turn of the conversation. Especially not any reference to Slade.

"Yes, yes, that's right. He was a junior partner years ago. Then went out on his own. Moved to Denver. But he still throws us a bone once in a while. So, I've been thinking. Wouldn't it be a plum to nail down the corporate account, steal it away from that Denver firm he deals with?" Chuck's eyes had sparked with a competitive fire Jamie hadn't witnessed in a while.

"I thought you were going to retire."

"In a couple of years, yes," he'd admitted, winking at her. "But why not go out in a blaze, hmm? It'll only make my share of the firm worth more, hence my retirement . . . we could buy a sailboat and sail to Tahiti or Fiji or —"

"I'll still have a job."

"Not if you marry me."

She'd squirmed. Chuck had been pressuring her lately and she wasn't sure what she

58

wanted to do with the rest of her life. There had been a time when she'd thought that enough money could buy happiness, that the reason Slade McCafferty hadn't been interested in her was because she was poor, from the wrong side of the tracks, and didn't have the social status of Sue Ellen Tisdale. But over the years she'd changed her opinion about financial success and its rewards. She'd met plenty of miserable millionaires.

"Listen." Chuck had rapped his knuckles on the desk as he'd straightened. "Think about it when you're in Grand Hope. Being Mrs. Chuck Jansen wouldn't be all that bad, not that I'm pressuring you."

"Right," she'd said, and managed a smile.

"We'll talk when you get back." He'd said it with the same confidence he oozed in a courtroom.

"What a mess," Jamie muttered to herself as she adjusted the thermostat while, presumably, back in Missoula, Chuck was waiting, expecting her to get off the fence and accept his proposal.

But she couldn't. Not yet.

Why?

Chuck was smart. Educated. Clever. Good-looking. Wealthy. His share of the business was worth a bundle and then there was his stock portfolio and two homes.

He also has a bitter ex-wife, her mind nagged. *And three college-age kids. He doesn't want any more.*

Jamie thought of Randi McCafferty and her newborn son, the way the baby's eyes had twinkled in adoration at his mother. Her heartstrings tugged. God, how she wanted a baby of her own, a baby to love. Could she marry Chuck, become a step-mother to nearly grown children, never raise a daughter or son of her own, one she conceived with a husband who made her heart pound and brought a smile to her lips? For a second Slade's face flashed through Jamie's mind. "Oh, stop it," she growled at herself in frustration. Just because she'd been thrown back here and had to face him, she'd started fantasizing. "You're pathetic, Parsons. Pa-thet-ic." She started to unpack the groceries, but couldn't forget how surprised she'd been at Slade's easy manner with his twin nieces and tiny nephew. Who would have thought?

Ironic, she thought, touching her flat abdomen. But, once upon a time . . .

"Don't even go there," she chastised herself, stocking the cupboard with a few cans of soup and a box of crackers, then stuffing a quart of milk and jug of orange

60

juice into the old refrigerator.

She remembered turning into the lane of the Flying M this afternoon. Her nerves had been stretched tight as piano wire, her hands sweating inside her gloves. But that had been just the start of it. Finally facing Slade again — oh, Lord, *that* had been the worst; more difficult than she'd even imagined.

He'd changed in the past fifteen years. His body had filled out, his shoulders were broader, his chest wider, though his hips were as lean as she remembered. At that thought, she colored, remembering the first time she'd seen him without clothes — at the swimming hole when he'd yanked off his cutoffs, revealing that he hadn't bothered wearing any underwear. She'd glimpsed white buttocks that had contrasted to his tanned back and muscular legs, and caught sight of something more, a part of male anatomy she'd never seen before.

Oh, God, she'd been such an innocent. Of course he'd changed physically. Hard-living and years had a way of doing that to a body. Slade's face was more angular than it had been; a thin scar ran down one side of his face, but his eyes were still as blue as a Montana sky.

She'd noticed that he'd limped slightly.

And there was something in his expression, a darkness in his eyes, that betrayed him, a shadow of pain. Okay, so he had his war wounds; some more visible than others. Didn't everyone? She folded the grocery sack and slipped it into the pantry.

She couldn't help but wonder what had happened between Sue Ellen and him, though she imagined Sue Ellen was just one of dozens. The McCafferty boys had been legendary in their conquests. Hadn't she been one?

"Who cares," she growled as she picked up her coat and hung it in the hall closet where Nana's vacuum cleaner still stood guard. All the McCafferty boys had been hellions, teenagers who had disregarded the law. Slade had been no exception. While Thorne had been an athlete, and toed the line more than either of his brothers, Matt had been rumored to be a lady-killer with his lazy smile and rodeo daring, and Slade had gained the reputation of a daredevil, a boy who'd fearlessly climbed the most jagged peaks, kayaked down raging rivers and skied to the extreme on the most treacherous slopes — all of which had been accomplished over his father's vehement protests.

But it had been a thousand years ago.

She'd been a rebellious girl trying to fit in. Not a grown woman with a law degree. Sensible, she reminded herself. These days she was *sensible*.

And sometimes she hated it.

"Don't lecture me," Randi ordered as Slade walked into the den. She was seated at Thorne's computer, glasses propped on the end of her nose, the baby sleeping in a playpen in the corner.

"Did I say a word?"

"You didn't have to. I can see it in your face. You're an open book, Slade."

"Like hell." He propped a hip against the edge of the desk. "I think you and I need to clear the air."

The corners of her mouth tightened a fraction. "Just a sec." Her fingers flew over the keyboard. "You can't believe how much e-mail I've collected . . ." With a wry smile, she clicked off and added, "It's great to be loved. Now, as I was saying, don't start in on me about the baby's father. It's my business. So if that's what you mean by 'clearing the air,' let's just keep it foggy."

"Someone tried to kill you."

"So you keep reminding me, over and over." Something darkened her eyes for a heartbeat. Fear? Anger? He couldn't tell, and the shadow quickly disappeared. Standing slightly, she leaned over the desk, pushing aside a cup of pens and pencils. "I get enough advice from Thorne. And Nicole. And Matt and even Juanita." Pointing an accusing finger at his nose, she said, "From you, I expect understanding."

"I don't know what you're asking me to understand."

"That I need some space. Some privacy. Come on, Slade, you know what it's like for the whole damned family to be talking about you, worrying about you, clucking around like a bunch of hens. It's enough to drive a sane person crazy. That's why you and I both moved away from Grand Hope in the first place."

"So who says you're sane?"

"Oh, so now you're a comedian," she quipped, smothering a smile as she took off her glasses and leaned back into her chair. Large brown eyes assessed him. "What's with that private detective?"

"Striker?"

"Yeah, him. I hear he's your friend."

"He is."

"Humph." She frowned, fluffing up her short locks with nervous fingers. "There's a reason they're called dicks, you know."

He snorted. "Testy, aren't we?"

"Yes, *we* are. *We* don't like being watched around the clock, spied upon, our lives being dissected. Tell him to lay off. I don't like him digging around in my personal life."

"No way, kiddo. It was my idea to bring him into the investigation."

"And it was a bad one. We don't need him." She was adamant. "We've got the sheriff's department. Detective Espinoza seems to be doing a decent enough job. Kelly should never have quit the department to work with Striker."

Something was going on here; something Randi wasn't admitting. "Is it Striker you don't like? Or P.I.s in general?"

"Both. Aren't the police enough?"

"No."

"But —"

"Kurt's just trying to help us find the bastard who wants you dead. You might be a little more helpful, you know. It's like you're hiding something."

"What?"

"You tell me."

"I would if I could," she snapped. "But that's just not possible right now. However, if I remember anything, anything at all, you'll be the first to know."

"Yeah, right. Then try concentrating on something besides people I dated fifteen years ago."

Randi's eyes narrowed. "It bothers you, doesn't it? What happened with Jamie?"

"I haven't thought about it much."

"Until now." His sister's smile was nearly wicked. "What are you going to do about it?"

"Nothing," he said, knowing as the word passed his teeth it was a lie. Jamie had gotten to him. Already. And he felt an unlikely need to explain himself, to set the record straight about the Sue Ellen thing.

Or is that just an excuse to see her again? Face it McCafferty, you haven't been interested in a woman since Rebecca, but one look at the lady attorney and you've barely thought of anything else.

"So what're you working on?" He pointed at the computer and shoved his nagging thoughts aside.

"Catching up on a billion e-mails," she said. "I've been out of the loop awhile. It'll take days to go through all of these and I've got to get my own laptop back. This one is Thorne's and I don't think he appreciates me monopolizing it as it's his main link to his office in Denver."

"He's got a desktop ordered. It should be here any day."

"That'll solve some problems."

"Where's your laptop?"

She bit her lip. "I don't know . . . I can't remember . . . but . . . why don't you ask Kurt Striker. I hear both he and the police have been in my apartment. Damn." She raked her fingers through her short, uneven hair, and when she looked up at Slade, her expression was troubled. "I'm really not trying to be a pain, Slade. I know everyone's trying to help me, but it's so frustrating. I feel like it's really important for me to get back home, to look through my stuff, to write on my own computer, but I can't remember what's on the damned thing, probably just ideas and research for future columns, but I feel like it could help — that it might be the reason some psycho is after me."

"Maybe it is," he said. "Juanita said you were working on a book."

"So I've heard. But . . ." She sighed loudly. "I can't remember what it's about."

"Then I guess we'll just have to find the damned laptop, won't we? Striker's still working on it."

"Striker. Oh, great," she muttered as Slade left her.

In the kitchen, he yanked his jacket from a hook near the back door and walked outside. The late-afternoon sky was already dark, the air brisk.

Overhead, clouds threatened to dump more snow. Not that he cared. He climbed into his pickup, started the engine and cranked on the wheel. He'd drive into town, have a drink and . . . and what?

See Jamie again ran through his mind.

"Damn it all to hell." He threw the truck into first and reached for his pack of smokes. He'd always gotten himself into trouble where women were concerned and he knew, as the tires slid on a slick patch of packed snow, that he hadn't changed over the years.

He could deny it to himself up one side and down the other, but the truth of the matter was, he intended to see Jamie again and he intended to do it tonight.

Shivering, Jamie changed into soft jeans and her favorite old sweatshirt before she clambered down to the kitchen where she found a pan, washed it, heated the soup and crushed oyster crackers into the beef and vegetable broth. She imagined Nana sitting across the table from her, insisting they say grace, watching her over the top of her glasses until Jamie obediently bowed her head and mouthed a prayer.

It wasn't that Jamie hadn't believed in God in those days, she just hadn't had a lot of extra time to spend on her spiritual growth — not when there were boys to date, cars to carouse in and cigarettes to smoke. It was a wonder she'd graduated from high school, much less had been accepted into college.

"God bless the SATs," she said, smiling at her own prayer. "And you, Nana, wherever you are. God bless you." She left the dishes in the sink, then started cleaning, room by room, as the ancient furnace rumbled and heat slowly seeped into the house. She'd considered hiring a cleaning service, but figured the scrubbing was cathartic for her and somehow — wherever she was — Nana would approve. "A little hard work never hurt anyone," she'd lectured when Jamie had tried to weasel out of her chores.

Nita Parsons had realized her granddaughter was a troubled girl who had one foot headed to nowhere good. And she had decided she wouldn't make the same mistakes with Jamie as she had with Jamie's father, an alcoholic who had abandoned his wife and daughter two days after Jamie's eighth birthday. Barely nine years later, Jamie's single mother had gotten fed up with a rebellious teenage daughter who seemed hell-bent on ruining both their lives.

That's when Nana had stepped in.

And how had Jamie repaid her? By giving her grandmother more gray hairs than she'd already had.

"Sorry," Jamie whispered now as she rubbed polish into the base of a brass lamp. She intended to scrub Nana's hardwood and tile floors until they gleamed, paint the rooms in the soft yellows Nana had loved and repair what she could afford.

And then sell the place?

Inwardly Jamie cringed. She could almost hear the disappointment in her grandmother's voice. How many times had she heard Nana say, "This will be yours one day, Jamie, and don't you ever sell it. I own it free and clear and it's been a godsend, believe me. When times are lean, I can grow my own food. Twenty acres is more than enough to support you, if you're smart and work hard. I don't have to worry about a rent payment or a landlord who might not take a shine to me." She'd wagged a finger in front of Jamie's nose on more than one occasion. "I've lived through wars and bad times, let me tell you, and I was one of the lucky ones. The people who had farms and held on to them, they did okay. They might have had patches on their sleeves and holes in their shoes but they had full bellies and a roof over their heads."

Jamie had thought it all very dull at the time and now as she wiped at a network of cobwebs behind the living room blinds, she felt incredible guilt. Could she really sell this place, the only real home she'd had growing up? And what about Caesar? Could she offer up the roan to some stranger for a few hundred dollars? Biting her lip, she looked at the rocker where Nita had knitted and watched television, the coffee table that was cluttered with crossword puzzle books and gardening magazines and the bookshelf that held her grandfather's pipes, the family Bible and the photo albums. In the corner was Nana's old upright piano, and the bench, smooth from years of sitting with students.

Nostalgic, Jamie glanced out the window.

A shadow moved on the panes.

Her heart nearly stopped. The shadow passed by again and then, behind the frosted glass a tiny face emerged — gold head, whiskers, wide green eyes.

"Lazarus!" Jamie cried, recognizing her grandmother's precious pet as he jumped onto the windowsill. He cried loudly, show-ing fewer of the needle-sharp teeth than he had in the past.

Grinning, Jamie sprinted to the front door, pulled it open and flipped on the porch light. Cold air followed the cat inside. "What are you doing here, old guy?" she asked as Lazarus slunk into the living room and rubbed against her legs. She gathered him into her arms and felt tears burn the backs of her eyelids. When Nana had died, the neighbors, Jack and Betty Pederson, had offered to take in the aging cat. Jamie had never expected him to show up.

"You escaped, did you?" she said, petting his silky head. "You're a bad boy."

His purr was as loud as it had been when he was a kitten. "Like a damned outboard motor," her grandfather, when he'd been alive, had complained.

Now, the sound was heavenly. "Come on, I've got something for you," she whispered, kicking the door open and starting down the hall. Lazarus trotted after her. In the kitchen she poured a little milk into a tiny bowl, took the chill off of it on the stove and set the dish on the floor. "There ya go."

The words were barely out of her mouth when she heard footsteps on the front porch. The doorbell chimed. "Uh-oh," she said to the cat. "Busted."

She expected to find a frantic Betty or Jack on the front porch. Instead, as she peered through one of the three small windows notched into the door, she recognized the laser-blue eyes of Slade McCafferty.

CHAPTER FOUR

This is the last thing I need, Jamie thought. *The very last thing.* Her stupid heart skipped a beat at the sight of him and if she were honest with herself she would admit that her breath caught in her throat nonetheless. If she had any sense at all, she'd tell him to get lost.

You can't do that, Jamie-girl. He's a bona fide paying client now, remember? Like it or not, you have to deal with him and you have to be professional. No matter what kind of a lying bastard he might be.

"Something I can do for you?" she asked as she cracked open the door, then, feeling foolish threw it wide enough to let in a gust of frosty air and give her full view of the man she'd sworn to despise.

"You said to call or drop by if any of us needed anything." Snowflakes clung to the shoulders of his jacket and sparkled in his dark hair.

"That I did." She'd never in a million years thought he'd take her up on it.

"I think you and I . . . we should clear the air."

"Does it need clearing?"

"I think so." His eyes didn't warm. Every muscle in her body was tense. "The way I see it, you and I, we're gonna be stuck with each other for a couple of weeks."

"Is that a problem?" she asked, sounding far more cool and professional than she felt.

"Could be. I don't want anything from the past making either one of us uncomfortable."

Too late. "I'm not uncomfortable."

"Well, I am," he said, one side of his mouth twisting upward in a hard semblance of a smile. God, he was sexy. "I'm freezing my rear out here." A pause. She didn't move. "Are you gonna invite me in or what?"

This is going to be dangerous, Jamie. Being alone with Slade isn't a good idea.

"Sure," she said, pushing the door even wider. "Why not?" *A million reasons.* None worth examining. The faint hint of smoke and a blast of cold air swirled into the foyer as he walked into the small hallway. Quickly she closed the door and leaned against it. She didn't offer him a chair. "So, what's on your mind?"

"You."

She nearly fell through the floor.

"Me?"

"More specifically us."

"Us?" Her heart catapulted. This wasn't what she'd expected. The professional smile she'd practiced all afternoon cracked and fell away. "There is no 'us,' not anymore, Slade," she said, clearing her throat. "Where's this coming from?"

"Guilt, probably."

"Well, forget it. What happened was a lifetime ago. We were just kids and . . . and it's just easier if we forget there ever was. We only saw each other for a couple of months. I'm surprised you remember."

"Don't you?"

As though it was yesterday! "Vaguely," she lied. "You know, little flashbacks, I guess, but not much. It's been a long time, more like a lifetime," she said, gathering steam. "You and I, we've got to deal with each other professionally for the next few weeks, so let's just forget that we ever knew each other, okay? Let the past stay right where it is. After all, it wasn't much more than a blip in our lives."

"Bull."

"Excuse me?"

"It was more than that."

"At the time."

"I'm not buying that you don't remember."

"I said I do, some of it, probably more than I wanted to when I drove back here, but let's just keep things in perspective."

"Perspective?"

"I'm an attorney working for you. You're the client."

"Hell's bells, Jamie, we slept together."

"That's really not so unique, is it? Not for you. Not with the girls around here."

His jaw tightened and he took a step forward. "You were different."

"Like hell, McCafferty. I'm going to be honest with you, okay? There was a time when I would have done anything, *any*thing to hear you tell me I was different, special, someone you never forgot . . . But that was eons ago, when I was just a wounded little girl. I'm over it and I don't want to go back there and I don't believe for an instant, not one instant, that you've had even the slightest bit of regret for what happened.

"So just because I'm in town and you feel . . . what? Compelled to 'clear the air,' forget it. I have."

"Nice speech you're peddling," he said,

looking down at her. "But I'm not buying it."

God, his eyes were blue. "You don't have to. You can take it or leave it." She wanted to step away from him. He was just too damned close, but she held her ground, determined to show him that she wasn't going to be intimidated or bullied. Those days were over.

"You're scared."

"And you've got one hell of an inflated ego, McCafferty. But then some things just don't change, do they?"

"That's what I've been trying to tell you. And you do remember, Jamie. You're too smart to have forgotten."

"Flattery won't work — hey!" To her surprise he grabbed her wrist in his gloved fingers. Worse yet, she felt a jolt of electricity — that same damned charge that had gotten her into all kinds of trouble years ago.

"What will?" he asked, too close . . . much too close.

"Nothing! It's over, Slade. Don't come on to me, okay? Just because I'm here and it's convenient, let's not go there." She tried to pull her hand out of his grasp, but he only gripped her tighter, and her heart began to pound, her pulse race . . . She swallowed hard, reminding herself that this man was the cause of much of the pain in her life, that it would be incredibly stupid to come under his sensual spell once again. . . .

"Admit it, you remember."

"For the love of God, yes. I remember that we dated, but that's about it. No reason to lie and make it a bigger deal than it was —" she glanced down at her hand "— and you don't have to act like I was important to you."

"You were."

"So important that you threw me over for . . . Oh, wait a minute, I'm not going there, okay?" She looked pointedly at the gloved fingers surrounding her wrist. "Let go," she ordered a tad too breathlessly. When he didn't comply, she managed to yank her hand away. "Let's just keep this professional."

"Randi accused me of breaking your heart."

She froze. All of her poise threatened to seep from her body and through the floor. "Boy," she whispered. "You . . . you just get right down to it, don't you?" Heat crawled up her neck as her pride crumbled. She tried to shrink away but he grabbed her again, his grip strong.

"No reason to beat around the bush." The

sounds of the night closed in on her, the hum of the refrigerator, the ticking of the clock, the sigh of the wind outside, and the crazy beat of her own silly heart. She had to end this conversation now. Before she was seduced into thinking that he actually cared.

"Look, Slade," she said, jerking her arm away again but stepping closer, angling her chin upward so that she could stare into those hot blue eyes. "I don't know what you thought you would accomplish by coming over here tonight, but unless it's about business, then I don't see that we need to be talking. Consider the air cleared."

She eased into the living room and propped her rear on the edge of the couch as much to put some space between them as to brace herself. Folding her arms over her chest, she added, "Anything else?"

The house had seemed to shrink, not only filled by the man himself but by the memories of a misspent youth, a few weeks that had changed the course of her life forever. She reached over to one of Nana's end tables and snapped on a lamp.

"I've got a couple of questions."

Me, too. About a billion of them, but I'm not asking.

"Why were you assigned to our case? I thought Chuck Jansen was handling it."

"I think he called Thorne and explained that he couldn't get away and since I was coming to Grand Hope to put my grandmother's house on the market, he thought I could handle it."

"Is he your boss?"

She bristled slightly. "A senior partner."

"And you?"

"Junior partner."

He frowned, his lips folding in on themselves, a furrow deepening between his brow. "I never figured you for a lawyer."

"But then you really didn't stick around to find out too much about me, did you?" she snapped, then bit her tongue. She was the one who didn't want to talk about the past. Before he could accuse her of just that, she added, "If you want to talk about what happened between us, consider the subject closed, but, if you came by because you want to talk about the sale of the ranch, maybe we should go into my office," she offered, pushing up from the arm of the sofa.

"That would be a good idea."

She led him down the short hallway to the tiny dining room at the back of the house. She snapped on the overhead fixture and wished it had brighter, harsher bulbs, anything to keep the house from feeling cozy or intimate. "Could I get you some-

81

thing? Coffee?"

"Not without a shot of whiskey in it."

"Fresh out. My grandmother was a teeto-taler." She managed another tight smile, motioned toward a caned-back chair near the window, then took one herself on the opposite side of the table.

"For the record, Jamie? What we shared? It was more than a blip."

Oh, if you only knew. "I thought we agreed not to discuss this."

"I didn't agree to anything." He pulled off his gloves and unbuttoned his jacket as if he were settling in. "That was your idea."

Obviously he couldn't be budged. She took a new tack. "Okay, but let's keep what happened between us in perspective. It wasn't that big of a deal, right? We saw each other for six weeks, maybe two months at the most?"

He wasn't buying. "That can be a long time when you're a kid."

"That's the point, we were kids."

"But we're not any longer." He shrugged out of his sheepskin jacket. "I figure we're going to see a lot of each other in the next week or so, whether we want to or not." He was undeterred. She remembered that about him, how focused he could be. Stubborn. Nearly obsessive. It had appealed to her at seventeen. Now, it was a pain.

He hesitated, looked away for a second as if studying the reflection of the room in the paned windows, then said, "I thought maybe I should explain what happened."

There seemed to be no way around it. "You went back to Sue Ellen. End of story." If only she believed it herself, could dismiss her feelings as a high school girl's crush . . . first love . . . but there had been more to it.

A lot more.

Of course he hadn't known about the baby. Would never. There wasn't any reason to tell him.

"Listen, this isn't easy for me."

"Nor me." To diffuse the tension, she scooted back her chair. "I don't know about you, but I could use some coffee."

"You're avoiding the issue."

But she'd already walked into the kitchen. She heard the scrape of his chair as he followed, only to lean one broad shoulder against the archway separating the rooms.

"There is no issue." She pulled out a jar of coffee crystals. Oh, damn, she forgot there was no microwave. Nana hadn't believed in them. Scrounging around a cupboard she found a saucepan, filled it with tap water and set it on a burner. "It was a fling."

"That's all?"

"That's all," she lied. There was just no reason to dig it all up again. All the old feelings, the painful emotions, the anguish she'd been through, were long buried. From the corner of her eye, she spied Lazarus. He'd been hiding in the pantry, but had slipped through the door that had been left ajar to rub up against Slade's legs, doing figure eights as if he'd missed the man. "So you came over here, explained yourself, cleared your conscience and now that's not hanging over our heads anymore. Let's just forget it."

God, his eyes were blue. "Right." Sarcasm.

Time to change the subject. "How'd that happen?" She motioned to his face and the thin scar slicing down one side. "A fight?"

"Yeah. You should see the other guy." His lips twitched. "Not a scratch on him."

She couldn't help but laugh as she found a couple of mugs, rinsed them quickly, then measured dark coffee crystals from the jar as steam began to rise from the water heating on the stove. "I can't see you in a knife fight."

"I wasn't." He fingered the scar and frowned. "It happened early last winter. I was skiing."

"And you fell?"

"Avalanche."

"Really?" she said, thinking he was kidding again, but his expression had turned serious. "But obviously not a bad one. You survived."

"I guess I was lucky," he said, though she heard the irony in his words and noticed as he leaned against the refrigerator that the edges of his mouth pulled tight.

"There were others," she guessed, carefully pouring hot water into the cups, then stirring the coffee crystals as they dissolved. "You weren't alone."

A muscle worked in his jaw and he stared at the floor for a heartbeat. "That's right." The silence was only disturbed by the hum of the refrigerator and the clink of her spoon against one of the cups.

"You had a friend with you?"

"Yeah."

More than a friend, she figured. From the devastation in his expression, she felt a sliver of envy for this unknown woman. "Is . . . is she okay?"

"She died."

"Oh, Lord." The floor seemed to buckle. "I didn't know . . . I'm sorry." Her heart dropped and she felt guilty for having felt any bit of envy for the poor woman. The seconds ticked by, meted off by Nana's clock in the living room. "I . . . I don't know what to say."

"Nothing. There's nothing to say." His eyes held hers for a second, then moved to the window again. So that was it. The pain she'd thought she'd glimpsed in his gaze. He was still grieving.

She handed him a mug and she saw how much he'd cared for the woman, enough that he was still raw. Or maybe there was more than simple grief in the shadows in his eyes; perhaps there was a twinge of guilt on his part because he was the one who had survived.

"Do you want to talk about it?"

"Nope." He sipped from his cup.

Her cell phone jangled from the dining room. "Excuse me." Jamie switched off the stove, nearly burning herself. "I've got to get that."

Slade nodded as she swept past him and retrieved her phone from the table in the dining room. "Hello?"

"Hi." Chuck's voice echoed in her ear.

"Hi." Oh, Lord, why now? She cast a look through the archway to the kitchen where Slade was watching her unabashedly, as if it was his damned right. Turning her back to him, she wrapped one arm around her middle and tried to concentrate on the conversation.

"How's it going? You meet with Thorne McCafferty and his brothers today?" Chuck asked.

"Earlier. Yes." She nodded, keeping her voice low.

"And it went well?"

Professionally, yes. An ace. Personally? A disaster. "I think I'll wrap up everything pretty quickly."

"What about your grandmother's place?"

She swept a glance over the dust in the china cabinet, the walls that needed at least two coats of paint, the windows that had to be resealed. "That'll take a little longer." Looking through the window to the backyard where the snow shined silver in the moonglow, she saw the faint image of her reflection in the glass. As she watched, Slade appeared behind her, holding out a steaming cup of coffee. She turned, accepted the mug and her gaze connected with his for just an instant. A heartbeat. She lost the thread of the conversation.

"Jamie?" Chuck's voice brought her back.

"Oh, what?"

"I asked how long?"

"I'm not sure. I'm still taking stock," she said. "But . . . but I'll come back to Missoula ASAP."

Slade walked into the dining room again and dropped into his chair. The legs scraped against the hardwood and Jamie inwardly cringed; she didn't want to explain this particular scenario — that she was alone with the man to whom she'd lost her virginity — to her boss and the man who swore he was in love with her. It was just too complicated.

"I already miss you," Chuck said, and she felt herself blush.

"All talk, Jansen," she teased. "All talk."

"No way." He chuckled and her cheeks burned hotter.

"Don't suppose you talked to Thorne about sending more of his legal business our way?"

"Not yet."

"Well, work it in. Do it smoothly though. Start by doing a good job on this land transfer and . . . oh, hold on a minute." He turned, answered a question that she couldn't hear, then said, "Wasn't there something else he wanted? What was it?" A snap of fingers. "That's right. How could I have forgotten? The last time I talked with Thorne he mentioned a custody situation with his half sister's baby. Something he wanted cleared up, but I don't have the particulars."

"Neither do I."

"Maybe you should get them, forward the info on to Felicia. Do some prelim stuff, dazzle McCafferty, you know, show you're interested in his family, take the whole family out to dinner on the firm. Just play the game."

The game. She's was beginning to hate the game. "Don't you think he'd see it for what it is?" she asked, embarrassed that Slade could hear every word of her end of the conversation. She walked back to the kitchen, put some space between her voice and his ears.

"Oh, yeah, Thorne will. He knows what's up, and that sister, she probably will, too. The other brothers, I don't know. I think we already talked about them, didn't we? I think I mentioned that one of the other boys is a rancher, the other kind of a nothing, I take it. The loser or black sheep, I'd guess. Never has settled down with a wife or a steady job, kind of into himself the way I hear it."

"Is that the way you hear it?" Jamie couldn't keep the edge out of her voice as she turned in the kitchen and, from her vantage point, saw the squared-off toes of Slade's boots as his legs, ankles crossed, were stretched under the dining room table.

"Well, he's probably pretty sharp. They all are. The old man, John Randall, wasn't behind the door when they passed out the brains. The youngest son was probably just pampered and lazy." She thought of Slade, his hard edges, his fixation with extreme sports, his raw energy. Pampered? Lazy? No way. "Anyway, do what you can," Chuck rambled on. "Schmooze them, work your magic, bat your pretty little eyes, anything it takes."

"Anything?" she threw back at him, and he chuckled again, deeper this time.

"Within limits, okay? We do have a loose code of morals here at Jansen, Monteith and Stone."

"Very loose," she said. He was kidding around of course, but tonight it rubbed her the wrong way, caused her hackles to rise.

"I'll phone you again tomorrow for an update," he said. "I've got another call coming in and I'd better take it. I imagine one of my kids is out of spending money again. It just doesn't end. Love ya, babe," he said, and hung up.

She took a long, slow breath, then, trying to get her bearings again, stopped by the refrigerator and pulled out the carton of milk. "I think I'll doctor this up," she said as she walked into the dining room and poured a splash of two-percent milk into her cup. Pointing the spout at Slade's, she asked, "You?"

"Mine's fine," he drawled, then looked pointedly at the phone. "Your boss?"

"Mm-hmm." She tested the coffee. Not freshly ground French roast, but it was hot and not half bad with the milk.

"Among other things," Slade guessed.

"What other things?"

"I'm figurin' he's your boss *and* your boyfriend. Maybe even more."

"Is that what you figure?"

Quickly he reached across the table and grabbed her left hand. A few drops of coffee slopped from her cup onto her papers. "What're you doing?" Jamie asked.

"Lookin' for hardware."

"What?"

"A ring."

The warmth of his fingers was too intimate. He rubbed the back of her ring finger with his thumb, then let it go.

"I'm not engaged."

"Yet. But your boyfriend —"

"I'm too old for a boyfriend," she said quickly. It was hard to imagine Chuck, fifty, gray-haired and forever worried about his nearly grown kids, as a boy — any kind of boy. She wondered if he'd ever been one.

All his life he'd been so damned responsible. High school, the army, college, law school, then straight to a firm in Seattle before settling in Missoula. He'd married his college sweetheart and started having babies right away.

Obviously, Slade didn't believe her protests. "Whatever you say," he muttered, but there was skepticism in his voice, a hint of amusement in his eyes that bugged the heck out of her as she found a towel in the kitchen and dabbed at the spilled drops of coffee.

"I say it's none of your business."

One side of his mouth lifted into a smile that could only be classified as wickedly sexy. "We'll see about that."

Her foolish heart knocked wildly. "Is there a reason you're here — I mean a reason pertaining to business?"

"Nope." He drained his coffee cup and stood. "I just dropped by to see you again." Shrugging into his coat, he rounded the table — then, to her surprise, dropped a chaste kiss on her cheek.

She nearly jumped out of her skin. How could something so seemingly innocent, a simple brush of lips on skin, burrow so deep, make her want more? Her silly pulse fluttered as she pulled away and saw the mockery in his eyes . . . damn the man, he knew how he affected her.

"Don't bother showing me the door." He had the audacity to wink . . . *wink* at her! "I think I can find it on my own." With a knowing grin, he turned and was gone, boots ringing against the polished hardwood, the door creaking loudly as he strode outside.

Jamie walked to the living room and, as she parted the curtains, touched that sensitive spot where the impression of his kiss still lingered. Dear God, what was it about Slade that burrowed right to her very core? How could he so easily bulldoze through all her well-constructed walls to keep him at arm's length? She watched the taillights of his pickup disappear into the night.

Sighing, she sagged onto the old couch. Lazarus jumped into her lap, and she stroked his silky head. "This is gonna be bad," she predicted as the cat began to purr loudly. "Even worse than I'd imagined."

CHAPTER FIVE

"I *don't* need a baby-sitter." Randi glared at her brother as she hobbled toward an SUV that Larry Todd, the foreman, used when he was at the ranch. Keys jangled from her gloved fingers and she was slowly making her way through the soft snow.

"Do you have doctor's permission to leave the house?" Slade was with her every step of the way, ready to ensure that she didn't fall.

"That's another thing I don't need."

"Randi —"

"Quit acting like I'm a two-year-old. If it's so important that a doctor say I can leave, I'll just have Nicole do it."

"She wouldn't."

"I think she'd understand. As for you, quit treating me like a two-year-old."

"Then quit acting like one."

Randi rolled her eyes expressively as she reached the vehicle and yanked hard on the icy driver's side door. With obvious effort, she struggled to reach the handhold above the door, then winced as she hoisted her body into the cab.

"You're not ready for this."

"Sure I am," she insisted, settling herself behind the steering wheel. "Look, I'm going stir-crazy, okay? I just need to get out, even if it's only as far as Grand Hope."

"Then I'm coming with you."

"Super," she mocked. "My own private bodyguard." Her eyes met his. "You don't have to do this, you know. I'll be *fine*." Slamming the door shut, she waved her fingers at him then cranked on the ignition. Slade was around the truck and opening the passenger door before she realized he hadn't given up.

"For the love of God, Slade. This is ridiculous. Beyond ridiculous!"

"I need some things in town anyway."

"Sure you do." She didn't bother hiding her sarcasm. "Put on your seat belt. The last time I got behind the wheel it didn't turn out so well." She adjusted the seat and flipped on the wipers, then eased out of the drive.

She didn't look too bad, Randi figured with a glance into the rearview mirror. All things considered. The bruises on her face had disappeared, the wires holding her broken jaw together had been removed, as had the cast on her leg, and her hair, shaved short while she'd been in the hospital, was beginning to grow out unevenly. That was the reason for the trip. She wanted a professional hairdresser to trim her locks, give her some style, even if the result was a punk-rock do.

"I don't know why you're still hanging around," Randi mumbled as she flipped on the radio, pushed a few buttons and then, sighing, settled for a country-western station.

"Still have to sign the papers to sell the place."

"And when that's accomplished, what? You going to take off?" she asked as the SUV blasted down the long lane to the main highway.

"Not quite yet," he said, looking out the side window to an area they called the big meadow. It was now snow-covered, the creek that cut through the field frozen; only a small, sparse herd of thick-hided cattle wandered toward the barn.

"Don't tell me. Seeing Jamie Parsons again changed your mind."

His jaw tightened. Randi's observation cut too close to the bone. The truth of the matter was that seeing Jamie again had brought back memories he thought he'd forgotten. He'd lied to her last night, telling her that she hadn't been far from his thoughts. That was just a line, one so transparent she'd seen right through it. But she did intrigue him. Now more than ever. He wondered about her, about the wild girl hidden behind the sophisticated don't-mess-with-me lawyer attitude. Yeah, Jamie made things more interesting, but the real reason he was still at the ranch was to make sure his sister lived to see her thirtieth birthday. He'd decided to appoint himself her own personal bodyguard, which she'd figured out and hated.

"I haven't really decided what I'm gonna do," he hedged, fiddling with the knob of the defroster. "But I figured I'd hang awhile."

"Not on my account, I hope." She wheeled onto the main road and gunned the engine.

"That's part of it."

"Don't bother. As I said, I don't need a keeper."

He slashed her a harsh look that silently called her a fool and she reacted in typical Randi fashion.

"Believe me, I'm serious! As soon as I'm able, I'm going to take Josh and head back to Seattle." She arched an eyebrow and glanced his direction as she shifted down for a corner. "You gonna follow me?"

"I haven't decided."

"Damn it, Slade, just leave it alone."

He ignored that. "I don't know why you're planning on heading west so fast."

"Let's start with my job." She lifted her thumb away from the steering wheel. "If I don't get back pretty soon, I won't have one. Then there's my apartment. You know, the place I call home." One finger shot up to join her thumb. "I've got friends and a social life and —"

"— and no baby-sitter, no car. You still can't walk without a limp. And someone's definitely determined to see you dead, if you haven't noticed. Now if you don't give a lick about your life, well, fine, that's your business, I suppose, but you're a mother. That little boy back there depends on you and only you seein' as you're not telling us who his father is, so you need to keep yourself alive. For the kid."

"Don't tell me how to run my life."

But Slade wasn't finished. "The way I figure it, J.R. — er, Josh, is a whole lot better off staying at the ranch with people who love him. He's got uncles and aunts and cousins, and Juanita, and you can't beat her. She raised us."

"I'm not sure that's a recommendation."

"Well, the baby's safe at the ranch. Why in the hell would you go back to an apartment in a city full of strangers?"

He snorted and thought he saw her chin wobble a little as she gripped the steering wheel so hard her knuckles blanched white. "That's where I live, Slade."

"Alone. Do you have a baby-sitter?"

"I — I don't know," she admitted as the frigid countryside rolled past, rolling hills covered with snow. "I, um, I thought that if I went to Seattle, back home, maybe my memory would return." She stole a glance his way. "There are such big holes. Somehow I've got to fill them. I've got to find a way to remember and get my life back." She swallowed hard and blinked as if fighting tears.

Was she on the up-and-up? She seemed so sincere, but then, Randi had always been a schemer. And a great actress. He'd been fooled before.

"Do you remember firing Larry Todd?" he asked.

She gave it a moment's thought, then, sighing, shook her head. "No. I can't imagine doing that."

"Well you did and he was mad about it, let me tell you. Thorne had to talk like hell

99

to get him to come back to run the place. He'd been the foreman for years, you know. A good man. Why in the world would you let him go?"

"I wish I knew." Scowling, she frowned at the road ahead and chewed on her lower lip. "But then I wish I knew a lot of things." Faith Hill's voice floated through the speakers and before the love song really took off, Randi punched the button for another station.

"What about the book you were writing?" Slade asked.

Randi sighed and tapped a finger on the steering wheel. "I told you . . . I don't remember. But I've always wanted to write a book, that much I'm pretty sure of. It's all so foggy." Lines of concentration marred her brow. "I'd have to go home, back to Seattle, check my computer files, go into the office . . ." Her voice drifted away.

The wipers scraped away snowflakes that caught on the windshield as a radio commercial for a local car dealership blasted through the speakers. "So why don't you tell me what, exactly, you do remember?"

"That you dated Jamie Parsons." She slid him a teasing glance and he couldn't help but smile. Randi, for being a royal pain in the backside, was charming as all get-out when she wanted to be.

"Okay, okay, but beyond *my* love life, is there anything?"

"Some things . . . but they're out of sync, kind of in soft focus, if you know what I mean. And it isn't that I just remember you dating Jamie, it's that I recall most of my childhood. You know, Mom and Dad, you guys as teenagers getting into trouble while I was riding horses and bikes, that kind of thing, but . . . then it gets fuzzy." She thought long and hard as the announcer on the radio gave the weather report.

Snow, snow and more snow.

Montana in winter.

So what else was new?

Slade watched the snow-drifted fields give way to subdivisions as Randi drove past the sign announcing Grand Hope's city limits. "I do remember some of the recent stuff," she admitted, driving past the old train station with its distinctive red brick tower and clock face. "My job at the *Clarion* and my boss, Bill Withers, and a few of my co-workers, especially Sara and Dave." Slade knew the names by heart. Bill Withers was the editor of the *Clarion,* while Sara Peeples wrote movie reviews in a column called "What's Reel" and Dave Delacroix was a sports writer.

"What about Joe Paterno?"

"Joe?" she repeated, her teeth sinking into her lower lip as she drove over the bridge spanning Badger Creek. "He . . . he works at the paper, too, I think."

"Freelance photographer. You dated him."

"Oh." Did she show a spark of recognition? Or was it his imagination? "So you're fishing again? Hoping I would tell you that he's Josh's father?"

"Just tryin' to help," Slade drawled.

She didn't reply, and when he brought up Brodie Clanton and Sam Donahue's names, trying to work them casually into the conversation, she rolled her eyes. Brodie Clanton was a lawyer. Sam Donahue a cowpoke.

"Don't take up private detective work, okay, Slade?" she suggested, easing into a parking space at the curb near the Bob and Weave Hair Salon. "You're about as subtle as a Mack truck." She parked, pocketed the keys, opened the door and slid out of the SUV and into the street where traffic rolled slowly through town. "And speaking of private detectives, be sure to tell your friend Striker that I've told him everything I know. Everything. If I think of anything else, *I'll* get in touch with him." She glanced over her shoulder as she reached for the door handle to the little shop.

Inside the salon three stations were filled with women in various stages of beautification. If that's what you'd call it, Randi silently chuckled. One of the patrons held her head forward while the beautician shaved the back of her neck, another had huge curlers in her hair, and the third looked as if she could pick up radio signals from outer space with all the pieces of tin foil stuck to her head.

"I'll meet you over at the Pub 'n' Grub when you're finished," he said, hitching his chin down the street.

"And I'll be a new woman."

"Just as long as you're a new *and improved* woman," Slade said with a smile.

"I'll try, but it's so damned hard when you start out perfect."

He laughed as she pushed open the door and started talking immediately to Karla Dillinger, the woman who owned the shop and also happened to be Matt's fiancée's sister. Her own hair was a mixture of blond and red and through the plate-glass window she cast a glance at Slade as if he were the devil incarnate. Though Kelly Dillinger was marrying into the McCafferty family, obviously Karla had deep reservations about her sister's choice. He winked at her and she blushed and quickly turned back to her client.

Hands tucked into the pockets of his jacket, Slade started down the street when he noticed the car, the little blue compact parked in front of a local realty company. One glance confirmed that the car belonged to Jamie Parsons. A quick look inside and he saw her seated at the desk of a petite blond woman.

He should just walk on by, but he couldn't. Not until he'd talked with her. Last night he hadn't gotten anywhere, hadn't explained what had happened between them, hadn't broken through her icy veneer.

Through the window he saw Jamie stand and sling the strap of her purse over her shoulder. She must've caught a glimpse of him because he saw her tense, her eyes lifted to his and then small lines of disapproval gather at the corners of her mouth. With a quick word to the Realtor, she walked to the door and joined him on the street.

"You know, McCafferty," she said without so much as a hello, "I get the feeling that you're following me."

"Do you?" No reason to try to explain.

"What is it you want?" She was walking to her car now, using a remote to unlock the

104

doors. "And don't start coming up with explanations about the past, because we've covered that territory already."

She offered him a cold, professional, guaranteed-to-put-pushy-males-in-their-place smile, but beneath her icy exterior he caught a glimpse of something more, emotions that she tried to deny.

"I was just walking by."

"Right."

"I dropped my sister off at the beauty parlor up the street." He hitched his thumb over his shoulder. "Then I thought I'd get a beer, and saw your car."

"So you decided to wait for me."

"I guess." Leaning a hip against the fender of her compact, he watched as a couple of teenagers ran down the sidewalk, backpacks slung over their shoulders, snowballs formed in their gloved hands. Laughing and shouting, they hurled their icy missiles at each other before rounding the corner. "You act like I'm stalking you."

"Are you? I hope not. Because there are laws against that kind of thing."

"It's not my style."

Her icy facade cracked a little. "I know that. I just don't understand what you want from me."

"Just some of your time."

"I don't know, it's pretty precious. The current rate is a couple of hundred dollars an hour, but for you I've got a deal. I'll make it three hundred." She arched a reddish eyebrow, silently challenging him.

He let out a low whistle. "That's pretty steep."

"Oh, come on, you can afford it. You're a rich man. A McCafferty."

"Three hundred bucks an hour?" He eyed her up and down. She was wearing slacks and a sweater, a long coat and boots; her hair was twisted into some kind of knot at the back of her head. "You think you're worth it?"

"Every cent," she said, and slid into the car. "Don't you?" She closed the door and as he straightened from the fender, she punched the accelerator and tore away from the curb. He should take her advice and leave her alone. Let that be the end of it.

But he couldn't. Whether she intended to or not, Jamie Parsons had thrown down the gauntlet.

Slade had never been one to back down from a challenge, and he sure as hell wasn't going to start now.

Why had she baited him? Why hadn't she left well enough alone? Been coolly disinterested? Or professional? Or just plain civil? What was *wrong* with her? Ever since setting eyes upon Slade McCafferty again, she'd been acting like a fool. She couldn't stop her pulse from skyrocketing at the sight of him, nor could she slow her heartbeat. The man got to her.

Jamie tossed her pen onto the dining room table and glowered down at the brochure she'd picked up from the real estate company. Her mind wasn't on putting her grandmother's house up for sale, nor was it focused on the buyout agreement for the McCafferty ranch, or even on the mystery surrounding Randi McCafferty. No. Her thoughts were filled with Slade, Slade, Slade.

Which was just plain ridiculous. She took a sip of tepid coffee, walked into the kitchen and tossed the rest of it into the sink.

She'd managed to keep him out of her brain for more than fourteen years. Every time his image had dared venture into her thoughts, she had mentally drop-kicked it into the next county, never daring to dwell on what had happened between them, what they'd shared and what they'd lost.

Absently she touched her abdomen. Their child would be fourteen years old now, going on fifteen. In high school, learning to drive. Maybe a cheerleader or an athlete or a bookworm.

Or a hellion.

It didn't matter . . . if only the baby had lived. She would have raised it alone or maybe told Slade the truth. But it hadn't happened. The miscarriage had taken care of that.

What she'd shared with Slade, that little piece of one summer, was over.

He was out of her life.

Until now.

"Damn, damn, damn and double damn," she muttered, cringing a little as if she expected her God-fearing grandmother to appear and wash her mouth out for cursing in her house. "Oh, Nana," she whispered, "what am I gonna do?"

You forget that McCafferty boy, y'hear. He's no good. Wild. Never goes to church. Lord, Jamie, you're so much better than all those McCafferty hellions rolled into one!

Jamie had heard the lecture before and it seemed to echo through the chilly hallways of Nita Parsons's cottage. She was cold from the inside out. All because of Slade . . . *Don't go there,* she told herself as she rubbed her arms to warm herself up. Lord, it was cold . . . she listened and realized that

108

the furnace had quit rumbling. "Now what?"

She found the thermostat, noticed that the arrow designating the desired temperature was steadfastly pointed at sixty-eight. "No way," she muttered, notching it up a couple of degrees. Nothing. She tried again, pushing the indicator to eighty. Nothing happened. No reassuring click or whoosh of air. The dial was pointed to eighty but nothing happened. Knowing it was futile, she walked to the vent in the living room and splayed her fingers over the duct. Sure enough, not a whisper of warm air was blowing through the old ductwork.

"Just what I need," she muttered as she found her grandfather's old toolbox in the pantry and made her way down the narrow staircase to the unfinished basement. Lazarus, ever curious, shot down the stairway ahead of her.

Lit by two dim bulbs screwed into ceramic outlets, the basement smelled musty. Dust covered every inch of the floor and cobwebs draped from the low ceilings. The furnace stood in the middle of the room, a behemoth with tentacle-like ducts stretched to the far corners of the ceiling. It had originally been wood-burning, her grandmother had explained, but had been converted to electric sometime in the seventies. Jamie placed a hand upon its dusty side. Stone-cold. Not a sound emitting from the monster.

There were instructions on the side and she wiped the dirt away and shone the beam of her grandfather's old flashlight on the panel, then unscrewed the cover and looked at the workings. "Now," she said as Lazarus walked around the cracked cement floor, "all I need is a degree in electrical engineering." The cat meowed as if he understood just as the phone shrilled upstairs. Leaving the tools behind, Jamie dashed up the stairs, flew into the kitchen and snagged the receiver by the fourth ring. "Hello?"

"Jamie?" a male voice asked.

"Speaking."

"Oh, good. It's Jack. Next door." She relaxed when she recognized the neighbor's voice. "Betty and I, we got your message about you being over at the house. Now you're sure you don't need any help with Caesar or Lazarus?"

"I can handle them," she said, and decided she wouldn't mention the furnace.

Lazarus appeared at the top of the stairs. He rubbed up against Jamie's legs as she listened to the neighbor prattle on, the gist of the conversation being that Jamie was welcome to keep Lazarus as long as she wanted because Betty and Jack, who had two dogs and three other cats of their own, thought Jamie might be lonely by herself. As for the horse, Jack gave her specific instructions as to his feed, water and exercise. "He's not as young as he used to be and we old fellas like to stick to our schedules," he added with a chuckle.

Jamie grinned. "I'll keep that in mind."

"If it was up to me, I'd rather you have Rolfe with you, he's our three-year-old German shepherd, y'know, and one helluva watch dog. He'd be more company for you, too. More than the cat. Me and the missus, we'd loan him to ya, if ya wanted."

"Thanks, but I think Lazarus and I will be fine," Jamie assured him as from the corner of her eye, she saw headlights flash through the window as a truck pulled into the drive. A second later her little car was illuminated in the glare. "I'd better go," she told Jack. "I think I've got company."

She hung up and leaned over the sink to get a better view outside.

There, big as life, was Slade McCafferty. Again.

She strode to the front of the house and before he had a chance to knock, she yanked open the door. "Well, well, well, Mr. McCafferty," she drawled. "This seems to be

111

getting to be a habit."

"Does it?"

"Mm-hmm. A bad one."

He flashed her a devastating smile. "And you love it, Counselor, admit it."

"In your dreams."

"And in yours." His lips curved into a wicked little smile that caused her heart to flutter stupidly.

"Don't flatter yourself. To what do I owe the honor?" she asked.

His eyes darkening with the night, he held up three crisp one hundred dollar bills.

CHAPTER SIX

"This buys me one hour, right?" Slade asked.

"Oh. I was only kidding around. I would never —"

Quick as a striking snake, he grabbed her hand and curled her fingers around the cash, then looked pointedly at his watch. "The clock's running."

"Slade, this is a joke, right?"

"Take it any way you like."

This was getting her nowhere, so she stepped aside and he released her hand. "Fair enough. Since the clock is ticking, come on in," she said, "but you'd better bring a wool blanket. The furnace is on the fritz."

"Maybe I can do something about that."

"If you can, I'll be forever in your debt."

Blue eyes sparked. He glanced down at the money curled in her fist. "In *my* debt? Is that so?" A crooked grin slashed across his jaw. "I like the sound of that. You're on."

He strode inside and as she closed the door, he found the thermostat, fiddled with it, then looked over his shoulder at her. "Is the furnace in the basement?"

"Yes. The stairs are through the kitchen, right next to the pantry . . ."

He was already charging down the short hallway and through the open door with Jamie tagging behind. Ducking his head to avoid low-hanging beams, he made his way to the nonfunctioning behemoth. "Not exactly the newest model around," he commented, grabbing the flashlight and screwdriver from the open toolbox and flipping open a dusty panel.

"Anything I can do?"

"Besides pray?"

"Very funny."

"When was the last time the filters were cleaned or it was serviced?"

"Beats me."

"Humph." He tinkered some more and rather than hover over him like a useless female, she climbed the stairs and, after having secured his money on the windowsill with one of Nana's jelly jars, heated water for coffee.

Damn the man, he'd paid her. Actually had the gall to hand her cash. Well, it served her right for being so flip on the street today.

The two cups they'd used the night before were still in the drainer. With icy fingers she poured dark crystals into the mugs, then added hot water. From the basement came sounds of clanging, banging and clicking, but no familiar whoosh of hot air rushing through the old ducts.

"Try the thermostat now," Slade yelled up the stairs. "Turn it off, then on again."

"Aye, aye, captain," she muttered under her breath, but did as she was asked. Several times. To no avail.

A few minutes later she heard the sound of boots pounding up the old wooden stairs. Frustration tugged his eyebrows together as Slade appeared. "I give," he admitted. "I guess you're off the hook. You won't be beholden to me, after all."

"There's a relief."

"I'll bet."

"But you can't fix it?"

"No, ma'am," he drawled, finding a towel and wiping the dust from his hands. "I think you're going to have to call the repairman."

"Which is the same conclusion I'd drawn myself, but here —" She finished stirring crystals into the hot liquid and handed him a mug. "For your efforts."

"Futile as they were."

She couldn't help but laugh. "I won't hold it against you."

He snorted. "That's something, I suppose. I think I have enough black marks as it is."

More than you know, McCafferty. "We're not going there, remember?" she reminded him as she sampled her coffee, wrinkled her nose and pulled a quart of milk from the refrigerator.

"Your rules."

"My house."

"Until you sell it."

"Yes." Pouring a thin stream of milk into her cup, she nodded and refused to acknowledge that the man was getting to her on a very primal level, forcing her to remember how easily he'd seduced her. Nor would she think of what her grandmother might say to that sorry fact.

"Don't want to keep it for a vacation retreat?"

"Oh, right. I could leave my condo in Missoula for the change of scenery here in Grand Hope." She glanced out the window into the frigid winter night, tried to keep her mind set, attempted to ignore how downright sexy Slade was, how her heart raced at the sight of him. Lord, it was hard with Slade. It always had been. "Your idea's tempting, I'll give you that, but I was thinking maybe somewhere where the temperature is above freezing. You know, like Hawaii or Palm Springs or the Bahamas."

"Wimp."

"Sticks and stones, McCafferty. At least I'd be a warm wimp."

"So you don't want to keep it as a rental?"

"Don't think so." She set the milk carton on an empty shelf in the refrigerator. "I think selling it and getting out clean would be the best."

"No muss. No fuss." Serious eyes regarded her over the rim of his mug.

"Precisely."

"But in the meantime you could freeze. Let's see if we can get this place warmed up. Got any firewood?"

"I think so . . . on the back porch, or maybe in the garage."

He started for the door, ready to brave the elements for a stick of kindling and a log, but Jamie wasn't interested in any more of his help. A crackling fire sounded far too cozy, too intimate, and she'd already found herself enjoying his companionship far too much, looking forward to seeing him again. There was just no point to it. "I can build a fire by myself, you know."

"I'm sure, but since I failed Furnace 101, I've got to find some way to salvage my wounded male pride."

"Wounded pride? That'll be the day, Mc-Cafferty."

His lips twitched and his eyes sparkled blue devilment, but he kept whatever was on his mind to himself. He drained his cup, left in on the counter and, with a bad Arnold Schwarzenegger impersonation of "I'll be back," was out the back door, the screen door slapping behind him.

"There's no kindling," she called through the mesh as an icy wind swept inside and rattled the windowpanes.

"There will be. Got an ax?"

"I assume so." Rubbing her arms, Jamie added, "There used to be one. But I think it's probably locked in the garage."

"How about a key?" He stared at her through the rusted, patched screen and all at once the mesh seemed a thin, frail barrier between them. Standing in the pool of light from the single bulb on the porch, with his breath fogging, his skin flushed from the cold, he looked more like the boy she remembered, the boy she'd tried so hard to forget.

"That's a good question."

"See if you can find it."

She should just ask him to leave, tell him she didn't need his help, that a woman

118

could chop kindling if she wanted to. Besides, he was bossing her around, as if they were still kids. Still friends. If she had any brains at all, she'd keep her relationship with each of the McCaffertys, especially Slade, strictly professional, but she wasn't up to arguing and the house was getting colder by the minute. She opened the pantry door, and found a key hanging on a nail by the shelf that used to hold jars of home-canned peaches.

She plucked the key from its resting spot. "Really, Slade, I can do this."

"You'll probably have to. Tomorrow." Slade opened the door and she passed the key through. Knowing she was making another big mistake, Jamie snagged her coat from the closet and made her way outside, following the path he'd broken in the snow.

By the time she reached the garage he'd already unlocked the side door and had flipped on the lights. He slid a quick glance in her direction as she entered, then focused on Nana's old car — a vintage 1940 Chevrolet. It had actually been Grandpa's while he was alive and Nita Parsons hadn't had the heart to sell her husband's pride and joy, even though she, herself, had gone through a succession of small, imported pickups.

Jamie ran a finger over a front fender. The Chevy had once been waxed every other week, but now the exterior had lost most of its gloss and cat tracks and dust had collected on the fenders, top and hood.

"This is a classic," Slade said, walking around the car and appraising it slowly.

"Probably. It belonged to my grandfather."

"And now it's yours."

"Yeah."

"Don't ever sell it."

Jamie laughed and rubbed her hands together. "You sound like my grandmother."

"I doubt it." But he grinned just the same and the tiny, dilapidated garage seemed a few degrees warmer. Dry wood was stacked in a corner and gardening tools, saws and hubcaps were mounted on the wall that stretched behind a long workbench. Jamie fingered the cold steel of her grandfather's vise, twisting the grip as she reminded herself not to fall victim to the McCafferty charm again.

"I really don't know what I'm going to do with the car," she admitted. "I had intended to sell everything. The house, the furniture . . . this." She rapped her fingers on the hood, then rubbed out a spot of dirt on one headlight. "Even Caesar."

"Caesar?" Slade repeated, and then, as he remembered, a grin stretched across his face. "He's still alive?"

"And kicking."

Slade nodded. "Good for him." Leaning jeans-clad hips against one fender, he eyed Jamie. "You'd really sell your horse?"

Guilt cinched tight around her heart but she tried to make light of it. "He wouldn't fit in my condo. Besides, I don't think he's house trained."

"The girl I used to know would never have sold him."

"The girl you used to know grew up," she countered, but didn't add how much he'd influenced the rate with which she'd catapulted into womanhood. Being pregnant and jilted had a way of crushing girlhood dreams.

"That she did," he said, and she felt the weight of his gaze slide slowly from her toes upward, past her hips, waist and breasts, only to stop at her own eyes. She swallowed hard, refused to glance away. "You look good, Jamie. You're a beautiful woman."

She warmed under the compliment, but didn't let her silly feminine heart take flight. "Thanks, but . . . let's cut through all this, okay? If you're trying to come on to me, Slade, it's not going to work." She stopped

121

fiddling with the vise. "I learned a long time ago that you can never go back. That's why I'm selling this house and yes, the horse, and probably the car. I pride myself in not wallowing in nostalgia."

"A businesswoman through and through."

"Yes."

"So you never married?"

"Not that it's any of your business," she reminded him.

"No kids?"

Her heart twisted. She had to force the word past her lips. "None."

"But the boyfriend, the senior partner, he's going to give you some?"

She didn't reply.

"Touchy subject?"

"Personal."

"Let me guess." He walked to the woodpile, selected a dusty chunk of pine. "He doesn't want any."

"Chuck's got three kids already. They're in college — well, the youngest one hasn't graduated from high school yet, but . . . wait a minute." She shook her head. "Why am I telling you this? As I said, it's none of your business."

"But this is my hour, remember? I've already paid for it."

Rather than comment, she sent him a look

that would cut through stone.

He got the hint. Rapping his knuckles on the hood, he said, "Just for the record, you should keep this as an investment."

"So now you're a financial analyst?"

"Jack-of-all-trades. Master of none. Today, I'm a furnace repairman and stockbroker."

His self-deprecating smile touched a forbidden part of her heart and she forced herself behind her carefully constructed barriers against this man. Emotionally he was a nightmare to her. Despite all her warnings, all of the pain, she still reacted to him, still wondered what would be the harm in letting him kiss her and touch her . . .

Oh, God. She cleared her throat and ignored the heat suddenly rushing through her blood. What had they been talking about . . . oh, yes . . .

"You're a repairman? Not much of one tonight."

White teeth flashed. "But a helluva lot better than I am as a financial analyst."

"Is that so?"

"Yep. I can guarantee you a fire, though. I'm a master craftsman when it comes to that. It's my primitive side."

"Cro-Magnon or Neanderthal?"

"Take your pick." He found an ax near the door and pulled it from the wall.

"How about a little of both?"

"Whatever floats your boat." He set the piece of pine on a scarred chopping block and swung the ax down hard.

Crack!

The chunk of pine split, the two pieces tumbling to the old cement floor. He picked up one of the pieces, set it on the block, then swung again. Wood splintered. Kindling clattered noisily to the floor. "What did I tell you? A master craftsman, here."

He grabbed another piece and set to work. Within minutes there was a pile of kindling near the door and the air inside the garage was filled with the scent of dry wood and disturbed dust.

"Enough?"

"Plenty. Thanks."

"No problem." He hung the ax back on the wall, grabbed an armload of the split wood while she picked two larger pieces and headed into the house.

"You don't have to do this," she said when they were in the living room and he, on one knee, checked the flue. Soot fell from the chimney.

"I know. I don't *have* to do anything."

"I mean, I don't think . . ."

"Are you trying to kick me out?" He looked over one shoulder.

"Yes."

"To quote the vernacular, 'it ain't workin'.' "

"It should."

He glanced pointedly at his wrist and she noticed the five-o'clock shadow darkening his jaw, the way his hair fell over his forehead despite the fact that he kept pushing it out of his eyes. "The way I see it, you still owe me a few minutes."

"I'm not taking your money, Slade."

Satisfied that the flue would vent properly, he stuffed an old newspaper around the kindling, flicked a lighter to the yellowed edges and as the flames devoured the Want Ads, he rocked back on his heels to survey his work.

"I think I should tell you about Sue Ellen."

"I thought we weren't going to discuss the past."

"That was your rule last night, not mine."

"Nothing you can say will change things, Slade."

"You don't know that."

"I do."

"You're afraid of the truth," he charged, standing, staring at her hard.

"No way," she snapped, suddenly angry. "I just don't think it's relevant. Not anymore. What happened between us —"

"The 'blip,' isn't that what you called it?"

"That's right. The blip. It's over. Forget it."

"I can't, damn it." Blue eyes regarded her. "Not since seeing you again."

"Oh, save me."

"It's true."

"There was a time when I would have clung to those words, Slade, but no more." His gaze drilled into hers, silently accusing her of the lie, and she wanted to squirm away. But she didn't. "I don't want to hear whatever it is you're so hell-bent on saying."

"Well, maybe, Counselor, just maybe, this isn't so much about you, as it is about me."

"Oh, great, so now I get to be your confessor? Now, after fifteen damned years, I get to listen to some weak excuse as to why you tried so hard to seduce me, just to throw me away when your rich girlfriend came running back to you? Well, no thanks. I'm not a priest."

"It wasn't because she was rich."

Jamie didn't comment. "Then she was more beautiful or more exciting or —"

"No way. She was . . . safe, okay? Safe. I knew what to expect from her. With you . . ."

"What?"

"You gave as well as you got, Jamie. Anything I dared you to do, you did it and then dared me right back. I thought we were on a collision course."

"That's what I thought you liked."

"I did. Too much. It was just too much. Too fast. Too hot. Too dangerous."

"You know, those should be my lines, because the way I remember it, you were the one always pushing the envelope, pushing me, convinced that we were both invincible." She stepped closer to him and poked a stiff finger at his chest. "You scared me, McCafferty, you scared the hell out of me and I liked it."

"Me, too."

The silence stretched between them. A hundred memories flashed through Jamie's mind. A dozen reasons to tell him to take a hike or to jump in a lake or to go to hell flitted through her brain, but she held her tongue.

Like it or not, he was her client.

As if reading her mind he said, "Yeah. That's the way I remember it." His jaw slid to one side and his lips barely moved as he said, "But, no matter what happened way back when, the reality is that you and I are gonna be dealing with each other a lot in the next couple of weeks and we'll have to find a way to get past what happened. So . . . I thought I'd come by and set the record straight, okay?"

No, she thought, it isn't okay. Nothing is with you. But she couldn't let him know.

"Okay?" he persisted.

"Fine, Slade," she said, dropping onto the arm of Nana's overstuffed couch and trying vainly to hold on to her rapidly escaping poise, the poise that always seemed to elude her whenever she was near Slade. Damn the man, why wouldn't he just leave well enough alone? Why couldn't he leave her alone, and why in the world couldn't she stop reacting to him? "If you're so all-fired intent on unburdening yourself, then, by all means —" she waved her fingers in the air as if she didn't care "— spill your damned guts."

"Good."

No, it's not. Nothing good will come of this, she thought, but again held her tongue as she noticed the stretch of denim against his thighs and buttocks as he warmed the backs of his legs near the hungry, crackling flames . . . She tore her eyes away.

Don't go there, Jamie, don't!

But the man's pure sexuality was hard to ignore, from the slight cleft in his chin to the breadth of his shoulders. She remembered clinging to those muscular, sinewy shoulders, feeling the heat of his body, a mirror of the fire in her own bloodstream . . . she hadn't had thoughts like these in years, not since . . . Slade. Always Slade. Suddenly the room was far too cozy, too intimate, too close. Though it was freezing out, she wanted to throw open the windows.

He was staring at her. She cleared her throat, pretended she was in a courtroom, and tried desperately to keep the emotions swirling deep inside. "Okay," she said, hating the breathless sound of her voice. "Here's your big chance to explain everything. Go for it."

His expression turned serious. "First of all, you should know that I was never in love with Sue Ellen Tisdale."

"You could have fooled me." Oh, God, she really shouldn't hear this . . . couldn't allow herself to believe his lies.

Lazarus jumped into her lap and absently she stroked his head as the old pain of Slade's rejection, the dull ache of knowing he hadn't cared for her, that he'd used her, settled over her. It was silly, of course. Downright ludicrous. But undeniable.

"I fooled everyone. Maybe even myself," he admitted, his voice low. "It seemed the right thing to do."

"As I said, it's ancient history." She tried

to sound flip, but her words seemed hollow.

He didn't immediately respond, not until she looked up and found him staring at her. His gaze was intense, the muscles in his neck tight. For the first time she realized how difficult this was for him.

"The plain truth of the matter is, Jamie, you were the girl I wanted."

"*I* was the girl you wanted?" She nearly laughed. "Oh, give me a break. This is like some kind of cruel joke," she said, though deep in her heart a very feminine part of her wanted desperately to believe him. How many times had she conjured up just this very admission? But, of course, it was a lie.

"No joke."

"Whoa — just wait a minute." She held up a hand and shook her head. "I don't know what you're trying to do here, but it's . . . way out of line. You didn't give two cents for my feelings. If you had wanted me then, you could have had me. I was nuts about you."

"So it was more than a 'blip.' "

"A schoolgirl crush. A short one. Look, I don't know what's gotten into you, but this . . . this is crazy," she insisted. How long had she wished, prayed, she would hear those words he'd just said? *You were the girl I wanted.* How many nights had she cried herself to sleep hoping foolishly that Slade would come to his senses, that he would love her? That he would track her down, spin her around and tell her that letting her go was the worst mistake of his life?

Just like a poorly plotted scene in some bad B movie.

"Let's just forget we had this conversation," she suggested. "Whatever we had, it's over. Has been for a long time."

He frowned, looked at the toes of his boots and then glanced up. "If you say so, Counselor."

"I do."

"Then I guess that's settled." He started for the door, but as he passed her one arm reached out, grabbed her around the waist and pulled her to her feet.

"Hey! Wha—" The tip of his nose touched hers.

"You know what, Jamie Parsons? You're the worst liar I've ever met in my life, and that's not good, what with you being a lawyer and all. You're supposed to be good at twisting the truth around."

"I haven't lied —"

"Bull."

"Honestly, Slade —"

"You want me to kiss you," he said, his eyes darkening to a seductive blue that caused the pulse in her throat to pound erratically.

"What? No!" She tried to pull out of his embrace.

"You've been wondering what it would be like. If the old spark is still there."

"Your ego is incredible."

"Along with other things."

She couldn't believe he would be so bold. "For the love of Mike, give it up," she said, but she didn't pull out of his arms and hated the fact that part of her thrilled to be held so tight, that the scent of his cologne caused her heart to race, that the heat of his body caused her blood to heat. She flicked a glance at his lips. Hard. Blade-thin. Nearly cruel.

"Come on, Jamie, admit it, you want to find out."

"I think it's you who wants to find out."

"Definitely." His face was so close she noticed the layers of blue in his irises, saw that his thin scar was taut and white. "And we still have a few minutes left on my hour. We may as well make the best of them."

"By doing this?"

"Absolutely."

Before she could take a breath, his lips slanted over hers. Pressed hard. Touched her as no one else's ever had. She closed her eyes, gave in for the briefest of seconds, felt the play of his tongue against her teeth, remembered how much she'd loved him, that she would have given her life for his.

Oh, please, no. Pulling back, she said, "This can't happen, Slade. We both know it."

"Do we?" He was still holding her, his fingers splayed possessively over the small of her back.

Gritting her teeth, she slipped out of the embrace. "Yeah, we do. I'm not some silly schoolgirl with romantic fantasies about love any longer, and I don't believe in making the same mistakes I did in the past. You know the old expression, 'Once burned, twice shy'? Well, that's me." She leaned one shoulder against the wall and told herself it wasn't to steady her suddenly weak knees.

"And you think I'll burn you?"

"Damn straight." On legs more unsteady than they should have been, she strode into the kitchen, retrieved the damned hundred dollar bills from the windowsill and marched back to the living room. "Our time is up," she said, stuffing the bills into the pocket of his jacket. "It has been for years."

He reached for the money as if to give it back to her, but she held up a palm to stop him. "Don't even think about it."

His smile was pure evil. "You're a hard woman, Counselor."

"And I pride myself on it."

Blue eyes mocked her and she realized she'd inadvertently thrown him a challenge. "What's the quote? 'Pride goeth before a fall'? Something like that?"

"You are a bastard, you know."

"And *I* pride myself on that."

Folding her arms across her chest, she said, "Not only a bastard, but insufferable, as well."

"So I've been told." He winked at her as he walked to the door.

So cocky. As if he knew he was getting to her.

Grinning as if her discomfiture amused the hell out of him, he opened the door and drawled, " 'Evenin', Counselor. Sleep well."

"I will."

"Alone?"

"That's the way I want it." Cold air seeped into the house.

"Is it?" He hesitated. "I wonder."

"Don't," she suggested, cutting the distance between them with quick steps. She wasn't going to let him get the best of her. "And for the record, it's Neanderthal."

"What?"

"You didn't know if you were Cro-

Magnon or Neanderthal a little while earlier. I thought I'd clear it up for you."

"Much obliged," he mocked as he slipped through the door and closed it firmly behind him.

"And good riddance," she muttered, glancing through the blinds to watch him walk across the snow-crusted yard to the spot where his pickup was parked. He paused to light a cigarette, the flame from his lighter illuminating the bladed angles of his face in the encroaching night. What was it about him that was so damned unforgettable? So sexy?

Angrily she snapped the blinds shut but it didn't help because, as much as she'd argued against it, she knew as she heard the sound of his truck roaring away, that she'd lied to him. As well as to herself.

It wasn't over with Slade McCafferty. It probably never would be.

CHAPTER SEVEN

So Jamie Parsons has a boyfriend.
So what?
What did you expect?
At least she's not married.

"Damn!" Swearing under his breath as snowflakes drifted from a leaden sky, Slade gave the wrench one final twist, then dropped it into his open toolbox. What the hell did it matter to him if Jamie was married or not? She'd made it clear that she didn't want anything to do with him.

A gust of icy wind blasted around the corner of the stables where he'd been working on an exterior spigot. What had gotten into him? Why after fifteen years of hardly thinking of her, was she now lodged permanently in his mind?

Why couldn't he forget the conversation they'd had last night? Forget the fact that she was involved with another man? Hell, hadn't he been through his share of women in the past decade and a half?

But he hadn't lied to her when he'd told her she'd scared him as a youth. She'd been so wild, unafraid to go toe-to-toe with him, that he'd worried they'd self-destruct.

In a way they had. He'd seen to it.

"Hell." Squinting against the wind and snow, he turned on the spigot enough to allow a thin stream of water to run onto the fresh snow and to see that the pipe didn't leak, then he replaced the insulating cap and straightened. He'd been checking all of the pipes running to and from the barns and stables, making sure none had frozen, just to keep himself busy. He couldn't spend every waking minute dogging after his sister even though he considered himself her bodyguard. Nor could he chase after Jamie, which he'd been considering. She'd lay him flat. And he couldn't go home to Boulder. Never would again. Because of Rebecca and the baby.

He glanced at the sky as if he could see God through the thick clouds. Why? Why take Rebecca and the baby? Guilt tore through him; raged as cold as this damned storm.

He straightened. He'd been checking the pipes for hours, all the while either worrying about his sister, wondering why Rebecca's image was fading, or thinking about his conversations with Jamie the past couple of days. He wondered about the man Jamie had been dating, the senior partner in the law firm, the older guy with kids. Last night Jamie had ducked the question about Chuck wanting to marry her.

Chuck. With a ready-made family and a secure law practice. A senior partner and probably stuffy as hell. But he could offer her a home, job, money . . . if that's what she really wanted.

Slade wasn't sure . . . there was a part of her that would rebel against the staid type. He'd seen the flash in her intriguing hazel eyes, felt it in the fever of her kiss . . . No, Jamie Parsons wouldn't be satisfied being a traditional corporate wife and stepmother.

But then, what the devil did Jamie Parsons's marital status have to do with him?

Nothing.

Absolutely nothing.

She'd made that abundantly clear. He turned up the collar of his jacket.

But she'd liked the kiss. Oh, yeah. She'd deny it from here to eternity, but the truth of the matter was that the lady, in the split second before she'd come to her senses, had kissed him back. Hard. Urgently. As if she'd been waiting for years. He'd felt it. That sizzling spark of warm, wet lips eager for more.

"Give it up, McCafferty," he growled under his breath as he snapped his toolbox closed. Even if Jamie was available, he didn't have time for a woman right now.

"Give what up?" Matt's voice stole upon him.

Slade turned to spy his brother, shoulders hunched, trudging through the snow toward him. Harold, paws slipping a bit, followed behind, keeping to the path Matt had broken through the icy powder.

"Never mind," Slade growled.

From somewhere in the nearby fields a calf bawled.

"Doesn't have anything to do with a certain good-lookin' attorney, now does it?"

Slade impaled his brother with his sharp gaze. "You've been talking to Randi."

"She swears you've . . . let's see, how did she put it?" He tapped a gloved finger to his lips as if in deep thought though Slade suspected better. His brother knew exactly what their sister had said. He was just enjoying needling his younger sibling. "Oh! That you've got it 'bad' for Ms. Parsons, that was it."

"What would Randi know about it?" Slade countered. "She can't remember anything about her own damned life."

"She remembers some things. And besides, she does write a column for singles. 'Solo' has a pretty big readership, so I imagine she knows a little about relationships."

"Then what about her own? Hmm? What about J.R., er, Josh's father? Who the hell is he? Why should Randi give two cents about my life when hers is a full-scale nightmare?"

"Ouch. Touchy, aren't you?"

"Yeah, well, yeah, I am. It's below freezin' out here and if you haven't noticed, someone's trying to kill my sister, and I've got to put up with you jawin' about my love life or lack thereof when it's none of yours or Randi's damned business." He pulled his hat lower on his head and picked up the tools.

Matt's dark eyes turned serious. "You've got a point there. Until we find the maniac who ran Randi off the road and tried to kill her when she was in the hospital, nothing else matters."

"Except your wedding," Slade reminded him as he glanced at the long drive and saw headlights cutting through the gloom of the afternoon. "It looks like your bride is here."

Matt's face visibly brightened and for the first time in his life, Slade felt a jolt of envy.

"See ya later." Matt was already plowing through the snow to Kelly Dillinger's little beat-up Nissan while Harold sniffed at the fence posts. As Kelly climbed out of the car, Matt scooped up a handful of snow and lobbed it in her direction.

The redhead laughed, hid behind her open car door and began furiously gathering snow, packing tight balls and flinging the frozen missiles in rapid succession at her fiancé. "You're in trouble now, McCafferty," she warned, firing yet another icy ball. It smacked hard against Matt's jacket, leaving a splat of white powder, proof of her dead-eye aim.

"Don't I know it?" Another snowball whizzed by his ear and he ran forward, past the shield of the door, and grabbed her around the waist as Harold barked wildly at the excitement.

"Oh!" Kelly cried, but was laughing as Matt spun her off her feet and kissed her as if he never intended to stop.

Slade had seen enough. He turned away and carried the toolbox into the stables. It was good that Matt was finally settling down, that he'd found a woman who was strong enough to stand up to him, a tough, determined lady who, until a few weeks ago, had been with the sheriff's department.

Kelly Dillinger had given up her job to marry Matt. Now, she worked with Kurt

Striker as a private investigator. Together they were tracking down Randi's would-be killer.

Slade thought of Jamie Parsons — Attorney-at-Law. Would she give up her career for Chuck Jansen? Did she care for the bastard, or was she just using him?

What does it matter? Slade thought, closing the door behind him. Inside, the familiar scents of horses, dung and leather mingled with the aroma of dusty hay. The General, an aging chestnut gelding, snorted at Slade's approach, then poked his head from his stall. "How're ya, old man?" Slade asked, rubbing the horse's crooked blaze.

Nickering softly, the gelding sniffed at Slade's pocket where oftentimes he hid a treat.

"Nothin' today," Slade said, hearing the sound of Kelly Dillinger's laughter seep through the cracks in the siding. With some effort, he tamped down his jealousy. He had no right to feel this way. He was glad Matt and Kelly were getting married. It was time for ex-lady-killer Matt to become a one-woman man.

And what about you? Are you going to spend the rest of your life mourning Rebecca and the baby? Or are you going to get on with your life? Find yourself a wife?

A wife. Man, he'd never considered himself the marrying type, even with Rebecca and a baby on the way. He felt another slash of guilt because he hadn't really loved her, not the way Thorne adored Nicole or Matt idolized Kelly. He and Rebecca had been better friends than lovers. They'd met whitewater rafting, had enjoyed extreme sports together and had dated eight months when she'd found out she was pregnant. The accident that had taken her life had taken place less than a month later.

So what about Jamie?

Yes, what? His eyes narrowed as he considered. His feelings for Jamie had never even bordered on "even keel." No, he'd been passionate for her. Wild. Out of his head with wanting to make love to her over and over again . . . her appetite and curiosity had matched his own and never had another woman been so uninhibited as she had. Every other woman had wanted something from him. Including Sue Ellen and Rebecca.

"Fool," he grunted.

The General, as if in agreement, turned back to the manger.

Slade frowned when he thought of the other women he'd been involved with, too many to think about. The only one that mattered right now was Jamie Parsons. Even Rebecca's image was fading.

Absently he fingered the scar on the side of his face and listened as a mare whinnied softly in the darkness. *Rebecca.* Pregnant and dead at twenty-six. He closed his eyes for a second, took a deep breath and told himself not to step into that particular guilt trap, as it was laid open, waiting for him, always ready to spring.

Walking through the building, he reached for his pack of cigarettes out of habit, his fingers scrabbling at the pocket and coming up empty. He hadn't been with a woman since Rebecca's death. Hadn't wanted one.

Until now.

Until Jamie Parsons.

And he felt guilty as hell about it.

"You're coming to Grand Hope?" Jamie said into the receiver, her heart dropping as she twisted the cord of her grandmother's phone. The last thing she needed was Chuck Jansen showing up right now.

It would be complicated.

Messy.

And she didn't want to deal with him; not only personally but professionally, as well. Didn't he trust that she could handle the property transfer, name change and whatever other legal matters the McCaffertys wanted without him peering over her shoulder? "I thought you were too busy to get away right now," she added, shivering as the heat from the fireplace wasn't able to seep from the living room to the back of the house.

"I am, technically," Chuck conceded, "but then I realized that the McCafferty account is worth switching my schedule around, and besides . . ." His voice lowered and Jamie braced herself.

Here it comes, she thought with mounting dread.

"I miss you."

"Oh."

He paused. " 'Oh'?" he repeated. "That's all you have to say? Just 'oh'?"

"You surprised me." *Liar! Come clean.*

"The proper response is, 'Oh, Chuck, I miss you, too. I can't wait to see you. When will you get into town?' "

"I guess I missed my cue," she countered, unwilling to go there.

That was one of the problems with Chuck. As her boss, he was a great one to laud her accomplishments in public, to extol her "sharp mind." But when they were alone, he was often quick to point out how she could have handled a situation with what he referred to as "a little more legal finesse." He'd often wink at her, rap his knuckles on her desk and say, "Don't worry, hon, you're getting it."

As if she were a fifteen-year-old girl instead of a grown woman with a law degree displayed on the wall of her office. Or as if she weren't quite as bright as she thought. It griped her. "So, when will you . . . get into town?" she asked, refusing to be baited or to mouth the words he wanted to hear.

"Day after tomorrow. I've already booked a night at the Mountain Inn. I'll give you a call once I get settled. Maybe we'll go out to dinner."

"Maybe," she said, trying to force a lilt into her voice. But she couldn't muster any enthusiasm at the prospect of seeing him again. Ever since returning to Grand Hope she'd realized just how little they had in common, how little she wanted to be with him.

For months she had talked herself into the relationship, reminding herself that he was successful, wealthy, smart, in great shape . . . but . . . the truth of the matter was her pulse never quickened at the sight of him, her heartbeat didn't accelerate. Not like it did whenever she was around Slade McCafferty. She'd told herself that she was

146

too mature for those kinds of girlish feelings . . . but then she'd run into Slade Mc-Cafferty and realized she'd been lying to herself and all those things she'd thought were important — security, a man with a steady job, a responsible person with a stock portfolio — weren't enough . . . or maybe even important.

"Oh, I've got to run," he said. "Barry just walked into the office. See you soon."

He hung up before she had a chance to say anything else.

You should have broken it off with him, before *he showed up here. You've been meaning to end it for months.*

Getting involved with Chuck had been a mistake from the get-go. She'd started dating him out of convenience. He was older, yes, and she supposed he represented some kind of father figure to her. But they didn't want the same things in life and he expected her to change her dreams, to give up any thoughts of conceiving a child of her own, and that didn't sit well. Damn it, she wanted a baby, wanted to be a mother. Stepmother to nearly grown kids that were being raised by their biological mother in another state just didn't cut it.

She'd have to break it off with Chuck. And soon.

Before he met with the McCaffertys and figured out that she and Slade were . . . *what?* Ex-lovers? There was nothing between them anymore, no matter what Slade implied. So they'd shared a kiss, so what?

So your knees turned liquid when he touched you . . . So looking into his eyes causes your heart to trip . . . So the sound of his voice, saying your name, gives you a thrill.

All just stupid, leftover emotions from something that happened a lifetime ago. And yet those damned lingering feelings served to point out why it wasn't working with Chuck — why it would never work.

Rubbing her arms against the chill, she tried not to think about her reasons for accepting her first date with Chuck. She'd resisted for a few weeks, then agreed to meet him for dinner. She hadn't been seeing anyone at the time and he seemed like a perfect match. He was handsome, successful, and had a quick sense of humor. True, he was quite a bit older than she and in a different place in his life. Now, as she yanked her jacket off a peg near the door, she supposed Chuck Jansen represented everything that had been lacking in her life — specifically a responsible father figure.

"Shrink fodder," she muttered under her breath as she slipped her arms into the heavy jacket, then yanked on a pair of boots. After donning gloves, she grabbed the largest basket she could find and braved the elements. The snow hadn't stopped all day and she broke a path through several inches of white fluff to the little barn where she checked on Caesar who, tail to the wind, stood in the paddock near the stables. He greeted her with a whinny, and trotted inside, where she poured oats into his manger and scratched him between the ears.

Satisfied that he wasn't freezing, she made her way to the garage, then loaded her basket with kindling and firewood.

Her breath fogged in the air as she stamped the snow from her boots on the back porch.

Once inside she found Lazarus lazing on the back of the couch, close enough to the fire to keep warm. He yawned, showing needle-sharp teeth and a long pink tongue as she pushed aside the screen and tossed fresh wood onto the flames.

Sparks drifted up the flue and hungry flames licked the dry oak as she glanced at a picture on the mantel taken forty years earlier. Nana, Grandpa and their only son. Jamie's father.

She gritted her teeth as she picked up the photo in its tarnished silver frame. Leonard

Parsons had been a promising athletic boy who had turned into a handsome, hard-drinking, womanizing man who had been unable or unwilling to hold a steady job. He'd pulled a disappearing act when Jamie was in elementary school and her mother had promptly gotten involved with an uptight older man who had never bonded with Jamie and as she'd entered high school, had had no use for a headstrong teenager. Eventually, after one too many run-ins, Jamie had landed here in Nana and Grandpa's loving, if strict, arms.

Nita Parsons had been bound and determined to not make the same mistakes with Jamie as she had with her son. Hence, her chores.

"Now, listen, you're my granddaughter, and Lord knows I love you more than life itself, but you need to learn about responsibility," she'd told her headstrong granddaughter. "The henhouse, that's yours. You be good to my little ladies. Gather the eggs, keep fresh straw in the nests, give them oyster shell and corn and feed, let 'em pick bugs in the yard and you'll clean the mess in the henhouse — every two weeks whether it needs it or not — mind you, it will. Then there's the garden . . ."

The list had never seemed to stop. But

Nana had been fair and paid her grand-daughter each Sunday evening, rationalizing that Jamie would spend the money more wisely if she was given her wages at the beginning of the week rather than near the weekend, where, Nana knew, trouble could tempt.

Jamie had resented her chores at the time, but now realized the hard work of keeping up the little farm — whether it had been learning to put up jam, taking care of the cackling hens or reshingling the garage — had not only taught her skills, but also kept her busy, tired, and walking the straight and narrow.

It hadn't worked entirely and Jamie's fascination with Slade McCafferty had been the result. A daredevil who defied convention, a rebel after her own rebellious heart, Jamie had stupidly fallen head over heels. When he'd kissed her, she'd melted. When he'd reached beneath her blouse into her bra, she'd been exhilarated. When he'd slid her jeans off her tanned legs, she hadn't resisted.

Oh, no, she thought now, pulling back the old gauze curtain and gazing at the blanket of snow on the bare branches of the aspens in the front yard. She'd given herself willingly, beneath a bright Montana sun in a field of tall grass and wildflowers. Slade's body had been tanned and taut, smooth skin tight over defined muscles, dark hair sprouting from a rock-hard chest. The day had been warm, his body hot, her virginity ripe for the taking.

They'd come close before, but she'd always resisted. That afternoon as a few lazy clouds drifted across a blue sky and the sounds of the creek echoed through the canyon nearby, she'd closed her ears to the voices of denial reverberating through her head. She'd drunk a little wine, just enough to lose what little inhibitions she'd had, and given in to the glorious sensations singing through her body. His hands against her sun-warmed skin were magical. His lips, sensual fire. His words, intoxicating.

"Goodness, you're something," he'd whispered, looking down at her breasts, pink tipped against the white skin forever covered by the top of her swimsuit. He'd leaned down and slowly kissed each rosy bud, taking his time, gently pulling back his head and tugging until a throb of hunger made her achingly aware of that private spot between her legs. "Beautiful. So . . . so damned beautiful." He'd kissed her lips and his hands slid over her flat abdomen to the mound of curls where her legs came together. "I've never seen a girl as pretty as you."

Somewhere in the back of her mind she'd thought he might be lying, but she'd ignored that horrid little idea. His hand had slipped lower, found her, and she'd froze.

"Easy now," he'd whispered gently. "Just relax . . ." His lips, tasting of wine, were upon hers again and he'd kissed her long and slow, all the while his fingers explored, touched, gently probed, until she'd felt hot and moist and been aching for more. "That's it. That's my girl," he'd said as she'd started to move with his touch, her hips lifting, the ache in her intensifying. "Let me love you, Jamie."

The words had brought tears to her eyes.

"Please." His lips, against her ear, allowed his tongue to trace the shell. "I won't hurt you."

Oh, but you might, she remembered thinking vaguely as he'd begun to kiss her neck and the tops of her bare shoulders.

"I'll make you feel good." He'd rubbed against her, his hot, sun-drenched skin, causing friction with her. "So good."

She'd moaned softly and he'd rolled atop her, his weight a pleasant burden. He'd nudged her knees apart and she'd felt his arousal, hard and long, as he rubbed her with it. Deep inside she'd been on fire and, as he'd pressed against her, levering up on his elbows, leaning down to kiss her lips, she'd given in completely, her arms encircling his neck, her mouth molding over his, her tongue seeking its mate.

With a groan, he'd thrust into her. Deep. Hard. Pain had seared through her and she'd jolted, her eyes flying open as he'd begun to move. *No! It wasn't supposed to be like this!*

But he'd plunged into her again and she'd felt a tingle of something new. Pleasure and pain. But the pain faded and she'd moved with him, sweat breaking out on her body, desire flooding through her veins. Her mind had spun wildly; she'd gasped for air, wanting more, fingers digging into strident, straining shoulders as he'd shuddered and she'd convulsed.

He'd fallen against her, gathering her in his arms as if he'd never let go. Which, of course, he had. In a big way.

They'd spent the next three or four weeks together . . . then Sue Ellen Tisdale had decided she wanted him back.

And that had been that.

Until now. She heard the rumble of a truck engine and watched as a van emblazoned with Grand Hope Electrical slid to a stop in the drive.

The cavalry had arrived.

But she was disappointed. She'd half expected to see Slade's truck parked outside.

The paunchy repairman carrying a clipboard with a work order was a sorry replacement for the man she wanted.

"Oh, God," she whispered at the realization. No way. She couldn't — *wouldn't* — want Slade McCafferty.

Not unless she wanted her heart broken into a thousand pieces.

Again.

Chapter Eight

"I'll look into custody rights when the father isn't around," Felicia Reynolds promised from the offices of Jansen, Monteith and Stone, hundreds of miles away, "but it would make my job a lot easier if I knew the father's name and how to contact him. From the sounds of it, he may not know he has a child, and there's always the chance that if he gets wind of it later, he could petition the court."

"I figured that." Jamie cradled the telephone receiver between her shoulder and ear as she pushed one hand through the sleeve of her coat. "But I doubt if that will happen unless Randi McCafferty contacts him or someone else spills the beans — you know, either a friend or a friend of a friend. Grand Hope is still a small town. Anything the McCaffertys do is big news around here. If the father of Randi's baby is a local guy, he would have put two and two together by now."

"But no one's stepped forward."

"Right." Shifting the receiver to her other shoulder, she stuffed her free arm into its sleeve.

"So either he doesn't know or doesn't want anything to do with the kid."

"Looks that way." Jamie's heart twisted when she thought of Randi's baby. All dimpled smiles and playful gurgles, with big, curious eyes and fuzzy reddish hair, the newest member of the McCafferty family had already gotten to her.

What idiot of a man wouldn't want to claim the baby as his son?

"I'll check all the angles."

"I'd appreciate that."

"It's a weird deal, though, don't you think? I mean, the buzz here at the office is that someone's trying to kill her and maybe the baby, too. God, how awful! Do you think . . . I mean, some people around here think the killer could be the baby's father, or even one of her half brothers, since she's inheriting the lion's share of the property."

Jamie bristled. "I don't know about the baby's dad, but it's not one of her brothers. I've seen them with Randi and her son. Thorne, Matt and Slade are extremely protective."

"If you say so," Felicia agreed, but wasn't quite done fishing. "What's this I hear about Chuck coming to visit you in Grand Hope?"

"Business. He wants Thorne McCafferty to transfer all his legal work to the firm."

"I think it might be more than that," Felicia suggested, and Jamie could envision the petite blonde sitting at her desk, looking out the window and twiddling her pen as she usually did when the gears were turning in her mind. "Chuck's got it bad."

"Bad?"

"For you. Don't play dumb with me, Jamie, because I know better, okay? I wouldn't be surprised if he popped the question when he got there."

Inwardly Jamie groaned. "You think?"

"He's been walking around the office whistling, for God's sake. Can you imagine that? Chuck Jansen *whistling?*"

"That is a little out of character."

"A lot. It's a lot out of character, so I expect you to come clean with me and tell me *all* about it, every minute detail! You know I get all my thrills vicariously through you."

"Of course you do," Jamie mocked. Who was kidding whom? In the three years that Jamie had known her, Felicia had been

158

through half a dozen boyfriends and dated men in between. Gorgeous and clever, with a wicked tongue, Felicia Reynolds was never at risk of spending a Friday or Saturday night at home.

"Talk to you in a few days."

"Promise?"

"Absolutely." Jamie hung up and snagged her briefcase. Thorne McCafferty had called earlier, requesting a meeting, so she was on her way. Back to the Flying M. And probably Slade McCafferty.

"If you break him, you can have him," Matt said, nodding toward Diablo Rojo, the orneriest horse on the spread.

Two and a half years old and full of fire, the Appaloosa snorted as if he'd heard his name; then, tail hoisted high, he ran lickety-split from one end of the paddock to the other. Snow churned from beneath his hooves and he whistled loudly, searching for the rest of the herd, and, Slade suspected, showing off. The colt knew he had an audience.

"Red Devil. Never was there a horse more aptly named," Slade said. "I thought you'd already broken him."

Beneath the brim of his Stetson, Matt's dark eyebrows slammed together. "I tried everything. I've never seen a horse so damned stubborn."

"More stubborn than you?"

Dark eyes flashed. "Maybe."

"I didn't think a horse existed that you couldn't break." Propping a boot on the lowest rail, Slade leaned over the top of the fence. He eyed the colt who was prancing and bucking, tossing its head and snorting proudly.

"Fine. I take it back. You can't have him. I'll finish the job." Matt slapped the top rail of the fence with a gloved hand, then pointed a damning finger at the horse. "You and I, Devil, we aren't finished."

The wide-eyed colt pawed the snow and stared at Matt as if he'd understood, as if he couldn't wait for another showdown with the man who was determined to be his master.

"Yeah, he's scared to death, isn't he?" Slade said as they turned toward the house, where, though there was still some daylight left, interior lamps glowed through the windows. Smoke curled skyward from the chimney and as they watched, strings of Christmas lights blazed to life, only to quickly die. A second later the eaves flashed with pinpoints of light again, then snapped off. Again the lights blinked.

160

The brothers glanced at each other as the door flew open and one of the twins barreled out of the house, down the steps, and plowed through the snow as fast as her tiny legs would propel her. She beelined straight at her uncles and as she closed the distance in her stockinged feet, Slade recognized Molly — the bolder of Nicole's girls.

"Dumb Buandita won't let me turn on the lights," Molly cried, throwing herself on the mercy of her uncles. Her lower lip protruded and she had to blink rapidly to keep snowflakes from catching on her eyelashes.

Slade lifted the little girl into his arms. "*Juanita* is giving you a hard time? I find that hard to believe."

"It's true!" Molly insisted, scrunching up all her features and folding her chubby little arms over her chest. "She's mean!"

"Mean? Juanita? Nah!" He touched his nose to hers. "But when she figures out you ran out of the house in the snow in just your socks, she'll probably skin you al— er, she won't be happy."

"She yelled at me." Molly's face was suddenly angelic, the picture of four-year-old innocence.

Slade hugged her more fiercely to his chest as he carried her up the rise toward

161

the house, Matt close behind. "Why do I have the feeling that you yanked Juanita's chain?"

"She's got no chain!" Molly insisted as Juanita, eyes round, lips pursed, gray hair springing from its usually neat coil, appeared in the open front door.

"There you are! *Dios, muchacha,* it's freezing out here and you without a coat. Or shoes!" She made the sign of the cross over her ample chest. "You'll catch your death."

Molly squirmed ever tighter to Slade.

"She seems to think you're abusing her by not letting her turn on the Christmas lights," he explained.

"Forever she is with the switch. On, off. On, off. The fuse will blow, and then Thorne, he will be upset because of his computer. You, little one," she said, wagging a finger at Molly, "will leave the lights alone. And you will not go out without boots and a coat." She looked pointedly at the four-year-old before a timer started chiming from deep inside the house. "My pies!" Turning quickly and muttering under her breath in Spanish, Juanita hurried down the hallway toward the kitchen.

"She's an old crab," Molly stated.

"I don't think so."

"I want Mommy."

"She's at work."

"Then I want Daddy!" As they walked up the steps to the front porch, Molly pushed herself out of Slade's arms, slid onto the worn floorboards and scampered inside, off to look for Thorne. Though he was legally only their stepfather, both girls had dubbed him "Daddy" since their biological father, Paul Stevenson, an attorney in San Francisco, was out of the picture. Paul and his new wife just didn't have time for two rambunctious four-year-olds. In Slade's opinion the guy was a first-class jerk, but then, most lawyers were.

His jaw tightened as he thought of Jamie, an attorney in her own right. She, he believed, was different. Though she tried to don the icy, all-business veneer of a corporate lawyer, he knew better.

He stepped into the entry as Juanita's voice rang clearly from the back of the house. "Leave your boots on the porch. I just cleaned the floors."

The brothers exchanged glances, then, grudgingly, used the bootjack before walking inside where the house smelled of roasting beef, fragrant pine boughs and cinnamon.

Nicole, with the questionable help of the twins, had spent the past few days decorating the house. Garlands of greenery had been woven with silver and gold ribbons and punctuated with sprigs of holly before being draped along the railing of the staircase and across the mantel. Colored lights glittered around all the windows and the living room furniture had been arranged to make room for a Christmas tree that had yet to be cut.

As Matt and Slade hung up their jackets, Thorne, limping slightly, ambled down the hallway. He was carrying Molly, and Mindy, the shyer twin, tagged behind them. "Striker called," he announced. "He's on his way over."

"Just Striker?" Matt asked.

"I think so. Kelly will be here later. She's over at the sheriff's department talking to Espinoza."

Roberto Espinoza had been Kelly's boss and was still in charge of the investigation into Randi's accident.

The front door opened, and Jenny Riley, a college student who looked after the girls, entered, causing Molly to scramble from Thorne's arms and both twins to demand her attention. "Just in time?" Jenny asked with an arch of one eyebrow at the uncles. "These little angels haven't been giving you any trouble, have they?"

"Not a second," Thorne lied, and Jenny

laughed knowingly. "Come on, girls, I've got a surprise."

"What? What?" Molly asked, jumping up and down while Mindy tugged on the hem of Jenny's jacket.

"It wouldn't be a surprise if I told you, would it?"

"What *is* it?" Molly demanded.

"I'll tell the both of you when we're alone, but it's a secret. A Christmas secret!"

"Oh." Mindy held a finger to her lips.

"That's right." Glancing pointedly at the McCafferty brothers, Jenny whispered, "We can't tell your uncles. It'll spoil the surprise." She hung her jacket on a peg near the door, then, carrying a suspiciously large oversized bag slung over one shoulder, shepherded the girls upstairs. "Come on, now, but don't say a word . . ."

For the next fifteen minutes the brothers discussed the ranch, Matt's upcoming wedding and, of course, the investigation into Randi's accident.

Kurt Striker, looking like a Hollywood interpretation of a rugged, lantern-jawed private detective, arrived half an hour later with the news that he'd located two maroon Fords that had been involved in accidents and had subsequently been repaired.

"Unfortunately, neither vehicle was anywhere near Glacier Park on the day of Randi's accident. The pickup was involved in a three-car pileup west of here — an old farmer was driving it on his way fishing. The other one, a minivan, hit a telephone pole when the owner's fifteen-year-old took it out for a joyride behind his parents' back."

"So we're back to square one," Thorne declared from his position on the couch.

"We'll keep looking," Striker said, his jaw set in determination. "Either the car wasn't repaired, we haven't found the right shop yet, or the work was done under the table, in a shop where they don't keep records. But we'll find it."

"If it exists," Matt said, as Randi carrying the baby walked into the room.

"You don't remember another vehicle?" Striker turned his attention to Randi and the baby, and if possible, his features hardened.

"No, and I think I've told you that before. If and when I do, you'll be the first to know," she said, sarcasm lacing her words. She sat in the old rocker, the bottom of her foot resting against the coffee table as she cradled her son to her shoulder.

"What about the guy Nicole saw at the hospital? The one dressed as a doctor, any news there?" Randi asked, as if to prove to her brothers that she was trying to be helpful. Matt propped himself against the windowsill and Slade sat on the end of the piano bench. Kurt sat in the recliner, but he was leaning forward, his hands clasped between his knees, his eyes focused hard on Randi. She returned his stare and Slade thought, for just a second, that he saw more than anger in Randi's eyes . . . it was almost as if . . . nah! She wouldn't be interested in Striker, wouldn't find him attractive . . .

"Kelly and I have been talking to some of your acquaintances in Seattle," Striker said.

"I thought you already did that."

"We widened the circle."

"To include?"

"Anyone you had any dealing with in the past couple of years."

"That's quite a task, considering how many people I come in contact with in my job." Gently she pushed the rocker, her hand rubbing her baby's back.

"We even got hold of your agent in New York. He said you were working on a book about relationships, that you were using information you'd gathered while working at the *Clarion,* maybe some actual case histories, that kind of thing."

"I don't remember authorizing you to contact my agent."

"You didn't. *I* did," Slade volunteered. "Since your memory is so iffy, I figured it would be the only way to piece what happened together."

"You could have told me."

"I did. But you were in a coma. And I asked Kurt to dig deep, Randi, to turn your life upside down. I figured you'd be upset, but I decided that was just tough. It's time to nail the bastard."

"But my book has nothing to do with it. Or my job . . ."

"Then what?" Slade demanded. "What does have something to do with it?"

"I don't know," she admitted, and some of the starch left her spine. Slade was reminded of her as a little girl, trying to gain approval from older brothers who didn't want anything to do with her. Now, it seemed, the tables had turned.

From his spot at the window, Matt shot Slade a glance. "Jamie Parsons is here." He couldn't help but grin widely, which irritated the hell out of Slade.

"Good." Thorne straightened. "I asked her over."

"Now what?" Randi mumbled suspiciously.

"Actually, it's not about you this time. I'm going to contract the law firm to work on

168

another property transfer here in Montana, but I'm sure your name might come up."

"Perfect, just what I need, all my brothers trying to run my life."

"Maybe that's a good idea," Slade suggested, pushing himself upright as the doorbell chimed. " 'Cause from where I stand, it looks like you could use all the help you can get." He walked to the door and cursed himself for wanting to see Jamie again. Tiny footsteps pounded, and the twins careened down the stairs.

Jamie was standing, briefcase in hand, on the porch. God, she was beautiful, her cheeks tinged pink from the cold, some strands of sunstreaked hair escaping from the knot at the back of her neck. "Come on in," he invited, offering her an easy smile and noticing the wariness in her hazel eyes.

Because of the kiss.

"Thanks."

"Get the furnace going?"

A smile touched her lips. "Finally. The thermostat was shot."

"Are we getting a Christmas tree today?" one of the girls asked, tugging on Slade's sleeve.

"Maybe later."

"You promised!" Molly charged.

"I know, but we have company now."

Molly glared pointedly at Jamie as if wishing her to evaporate.

"You said we could get one today," Mindy, the shyer girl, reminded her uncle.

"Okay, then we will." Squatting to be at eye level with the girls, he said, "As soon as I'm finished. Now you get bundled up, okay? No more running outside in stockings!" He looked up at Jamie. "Don't ask." Then he touched Molly's dark curls. "We'll take General out with the sleigh and get the tree."

"Promise?" Molly asked, her little face screwed up in disbelief.

Slade lifted a hand. Held up two fingers. "On my honor. Now, have Juanita pack us a thermos of hot chocolate and maybe some cookies, then get Jenny to find your snowsuits. And boots. But don't bug me anymore. When I'm done here, I'll take you. We'll find the best Christmas tree on the ranch!"

Molly's face burst into a wide grin and Mindy glanced up at Slade through her eyelashes.

"Go on!" he said, and they took off, running down the hallway toward the kitchen.

Straightening, Slade found Jamie staring at him as if he'd lost his mind. "I never thought I'd see the day," she said. "You?

Going out for a Christmas tree with two little girls? *In a sleigh?*"

"Well, Counselor, maybe there are a few things you don't know about me."

"Maybe."

"You could come along if you want." The thought of her bundled up next to him in the sleigh held more than a little appeal.

"I — I'm here on business."

"After business."

"I don't know. I'm not really dressed for it . . ."

"All you have to do is ride. I'll handle the horse and hauling the tree. Come on, you know what they say about 'all work and no play.' "

"It pays the bills?"

"Yeah, that's it," he remarked as Kurt, zipping his jacket walked through the hallway and out the front door.

"I'll call you later," he promised, then hitched a thumb toward the living room. "It would help a helluva lot if your sister cooperated."

"She's trying."

"Like hell. Talk some sense into her. Before she gets herself killed." Without pausing for an introduction, Striker stormed out of the house.

"Nice guy," Jamie observed, and it wasn't

just her opinion. Randi was beside herself in the living room.

"What an A number-one jerk," she raved, carrying the baby and, limping, making her way to the window as if to make sure that Kurt Striker was actually leaving.

"He's just what we need," Slade countered.

"Since when do we need a rude, obnoxious jerk poking around?" Randi demanded.

"Since someone tried to kill you and you can't or won't tell us what happened."

"Don't you think I'd be the first one to go to the police and explain who was doing this if I knew?"

"I don't know, Randi," Slade admitted. "I honestly don't know."

"You miserable . . ." Randi glanced over at Thorne and met an expression as hard and determined as Slade's, and when she turned to Matt, she swallowed back any further argument because from the determination in his dark eyes it was clear that even he was taking a hard line with her.

"This is serious stuff, kiddo," Slade pointed out. "I was willing to believe that maybe you were in just some kind of odd, single-car accident, but then someone tried to kill you in the hospital. You don't remember it, but I do. Damn, it was scary, so don't

172

argue with us, okay? The police are fine, but we need more. I've known Striker for years. He's good. He'll find out who's behind all this, but you've got to help him."

She gritted her teeth, looked down at her baby and then sighed as she saw little Joshua move his tiny lips. "Okay, I'll try," she vowed. "Really, I will, but there's something about that guy I don't trust."

The baby opened his eyes and suddenly began to fuss. All of Randi's attention was riveted on her son. "Uh-oh. Look who's getting cranky." She dropped a kiss onto his forehead, then nuzzled his cheek. "Bedtime for you, I think," she said, and winked at her baby. The transformation was remarkable. Ready to take on Kurt Striker and the whole damned world one minute, Randi became a doting mother whose only concern was her baby the next. She breezed out of the room, and Slade watched her climb the stairs. Once she'd disappeared, he looked at Thorne. "It would help if she would cooperate a little more."

"Oh, give her a break." Matt eased away from the window and tossed a log onto the dying fire. "She can't remember much."

Slade's gaze lingered on the stairway. "So she says."

"You're not buying it?"

"Nope," Slade admitted. "Not in a million years. I think our sister is hiding something."

"What?"

"Now that's the million dollar question, isn't it?"

"What are we gonna do?" Randi asked as she tucked Joshua's blanket to his neck. His eyes were already closed and he let out a soft little sigh that nearly broke her heart. Lord, how she loved him. She hadn't known that kind of love was possible, though her father had warned her enough. "Wait till you have yourself a little one," John Randall had told her one day before he'd died. "Then you'll understand what it's like to love something more than life itself."

It had been early spring and he'd been sitting on the porch and watching the spindly legged foals scamper in the field they called Big Meadow. While the mares had lazily plucked grass, their tails switching at flies, the rambunctious fillies and colts had bucked and galloped through the long grass. Her father had nodded to himself, approving of his wisdom. He'd grabbed her hand with long fingers and a surprisingly strong grip. "You think you're invincible, you think nothing can hurt you, but once you have a child, that's when you're vulnerable, when you experience real fear for the first time."

She hadn't really understood him at the time, but now, looking down at her baby, realizing that if she didn't stop whoever was trying to harm her, her son could be injured. John Randall's words had new meaning.

She thought of the baby's father . . . yes, no matter what she said to her brothers, she knew darned well who had sired her baby. And the bastard didn't deserve to know about him.

"I'm sorry," she whispered to little Joshua. So innocent. Someday he would have to know the truth, hard as it was. "I'll take care of you," she promised, smoothing his downy red hair. "I promise. I won't let anyone hurt you."

She turned and found Slade standing in the doorway of the nursery. His arms were folded over his chest, a shoulder propped on the door frame. "You got something you want to tell me?" he asked, and she felt a second's hesitation. Could she confide in him? Slade and she were the closest, not only in age, but temperament. And that was the problem. If Slade knew the circumstances behind Josh's conception and birth, he'd go ballistic.

"What would that be?" she asked, offering him a smile as she pressed a finger to her lips and turned off the light. She grabbed Slade's arm and propelled him into the hallway where she left the door to the nursery slightly ajar.

His lips pulled into a tight, unyielding frown. "I think you're holding out," he said, resting his hips on the railing of the upper landing.

"How's that?"

"Something's up with you, Randi, and don't try to deny it. You're talking to me, remember? I know you. This amnesia thing is all a blind. Smoke and mirrors. I think you've got yourself into some kind of big trouble and you're pretending not to remember it in the hope that it'll conveniently disappear." His eyes narrowed slightly. "I'm thinking that you've manipulated all of us — Thorne, Matt and me — even the doctors — so that word will leak out to the street via the press. You're a reporter, and you know how that works. You're hoping that you can buy yourself some time with the amnesia bit."

"Why would I do that?"

"My guess is because you're scared. Either you're protecting someone or you need some time in order to . . ." He snapped his fingers. "Is it about the book? Have you got yourself into some hot water over the book? Striker and the police have already questioned everyone at the paper and gone through all your old articles, even the ones written under the name of R.J. McKay."

"R.J.?" she repeated.

"The freelance articles . . ."

The name did ring a bell — a far-distant bell.

"Your editor thought you probably wrote them for some extra cash."

"I . . . I suppose."

"But they weren't anything that would get you into any trouble, nor were your columns, not that we could figure. So either what's got you on the run is —"

"I'm *not* on the run," she clarified. "I'm recuperating. As soon as I can, I intend to reclaim my life, pack up Joshua —" she hitched a thumb to the cracked nursery door "— and return to Seattle. I've already talked to my boss. Bill wants me back as soon as I can get there, so I'm not on the run."

"Fine, but you're scared. And you're involved in something dangerous. Is it the book? What could that be? Are you writing some kind of exposé on political crime or the Mob or . . . what? Or is it J.R., er, Josh's

177

dad?" He stared at her and she saw that he cared, really cared. Slade, for all his bluster and bravado and macho attitude, had a soft side, a soul that could be hurt.

"Tell ya what," she said, fighting the urge to tell him everything. "As soon as I remember anything important, I'll let you know."

He eyed her suspiciously. "Why do I think you're lying?"

"Because you have trust issues," she said, and he rolled his eyes. "Things are getting clearer." That much was true. "Just be patient, okay?"

"It's not, and patience isn't my long suit. But I'll give you some space, not much, but a little, and when you have a breakthrough or whatever it is, you'd better talk to me."

"Scout's honor," she promised, cringing a little at the lie. She would tell him. Soon. But she wasn't sure when. Or how. There were things in her memory that were fuzzy, some seemed to have disappeared entirely, but day by day, bit by bit, her past was returning. It was just a matter of time.

"You'd better not be yanking my chain."

"Why don't you forget about me for a minute? There are other things we've got to work out." When he lifted a dark brow, she said, "Let's start with the transfer of property. When Matt buys you out, what're you going to do with the rest of your life?"

"I haven't decided yet."

"Well, you'd better figure it out, and while you're at it," she advised, starting for the stairs, "you'd better pencil Jamie Parsons into the equation."

CHAPTER NINE

"So what you're suggesting," Jamie said, leveling her gaze across the desk, "is that the firm use all its resources to try to find out everything we can about your sister, pry into her personal life, dig deep, use private investigators, snitches — whatever it takes — to find out who's the father of her child. And in return, you'll throw us a bone, a little more business our way. Is that what you want to do?"

"Absolutely." Thorne leaned his elbows on the scarred wooden desk. The den was small and had never been intended to house computers, a fax machine, printers, scanners, copiers and a phone with several lines, yet it didn't seem cluttered — just compact and efficient. Like the man trying to convince Jamie that what he was doing was somehow benign. Thorne wasn't giving an inch. "The police are too slow. Striker's frustrated. Randi can't or won't remember anything that might help, and I have the feeling we're running out of time. Whoever wants to harm her won't wait to strike again."

"Isn't that her business?"

"I'm just taking care of my sister," Thorne insisted, his gray eyes steely with determination. "I would never forgive myself if I let her bully me into backing off and something happened to her or the baby. Don't worry, this isn't going to be behind her back. I'll tell her."

"That you bargained for her. Offered more business to Jansen, Monteith and Stone *if* they were able to unearth her deepest secrets? *That's* what you're going to tell her?" Jamie stared at the man in disbelief. "I'm just glad you're not my brother."

"She'll appreciate it."

"I met her. I don't think so."

Thorne's jaw hardened. "You don't have to second-guess me, just pass the information along. We're talking a lot of business to the firm. I've already got my eye on two potential developments in this county, one outside of Grand Hope, another on the way to Carver . . . and that's just a start. I've got drilling rights in Colorado and . . ." His face fell away as he leaned back in his desk chair and it squeaked. "Just have Chuck give me a call."

"I will," she promised, standing briskly.

He must have read the censure in her eyes, because his expression was suddenly not set in granite. "I really am looking out for my sister and her son's best interests. How would any of us feel if we hadn't done everything possible to ensure their safety and something tragic happened? Not only has someone tried to kill my sister twice, but the baby nearly died in the hospital from complications surrounding his birth. Bacterial meningitis."

Lines of worry creased Thorne's face and Jamie realized that be he right or wrong, he really was doing what he thought best, that he cared. Even if she thought he was going about it all wrong. He hadn't suggested anything illegal.

"I'll talk to Chuck," she promised, leaving the small office. What the devil was she getting herself into? The McCafferty brothers were all hardheaded and extremely protective when it came to their sister.

You're not getting yourself into anything. This is just business. Try to remember that.

But it seemed impossible. Especially with Slade. The other brothers were handsome, intriguing men, but even if they were both single, she could have resisted their charms. Not so with the youngest brother, even though he'd nearly destroyed her once before. Well, never again, she thought, squaring her shoulders as she walked to the front of the house.

Slade was waiting for her.

Leaning against a post near the stairs, arms crossed over his chest, amused smile curving his lips, as if he knew her recent thoughts and was hell-bent to prove her wrong.

"Have fun with Thorne?" he drawled.

"It was business."

"Business is his fun."

She arched a brow. "Is it?"

"Well, it was. For years, it was all he talked about. Hooking up with Nicole mellowed him out."

"I don't know if I'd call him 'mellow.' "

"Yeah, well, you should've seen him before. So." He straightened and hitched his chin toward the door. "Ready?"

"For what?"

Before he could answer, tiny feet pounded, and the twins raced down the hall. One wore a pink snowsuit, the other was dressed in yellow. Both wore boots and mittens. Eager, rosy faces turned upward in anticipation.

"Can we go now?" one cherub asked. She was jumping up and down, unable to contain an iota of her excitement, while the other one was all shy smiles that she cast up at her uncle.

"I think so," Slade said, winking at the girls. "I was just trying to talk Ms. Parsons into joining us."

Two sets of bright eyes focused on Jamie.

"Hurry!" the liveliest twin — was it Molly? — ordered as if she were a little drill sergeant. "We gots to go. Now!"

"Oh, I don't know. I don't have a snowsuit like you girls and —"

"And you'll be fine," Slade insisted, opening the door.

Crisp winter air slid inside. Snow was falling in lazy flakes and a tall chestnut-colored horse stood in the drive, harnessed to what had once been a sleek red sleigh. "It'll be fun," Slade insisted.

Fun? With Slade McCafferty?

Jamie didn't think so.

The horse shook his great head and bells attached to his harness jingled in the snowfall.

"Oo-oh!" one little girl cried, placing her hands over her cheeks. The other one was out of the door like a rocket, black boots flashing against the white snow.

"Come on, Counselor," he insisted, touching her arm. "What would it hurt?"

She thought of her heart, once so bitterly wounded by this man, considered her pride, how it had been battered, her self-esteem that had been pounded into nearly nothing. It had taken her years to get over the ache, and now . . . now she should risk it all again? "I'll let you drive." His blue eyes flashed with a dare and a crooked smile slashed across a square jaw dark with beard shadow.

She couldn't resist. "All right, McCafferty, you're on," she agreed. "But only if I can use the whip on you if you get out of line."

The smile stretched wider. "It's a deal. I'll try to be on my worst behavior."

He took her hand, and with the shy twin following, they walked briskly down the broken snow path to the sleigh. The impetuous twin was trying and failing to climb into the old sleigh. "Here ya go, pumpkin," Slade said, hoisting her into the back seat where thick coverlets had been tucked around the cold leather.

"What's in here?" Molly asked, pointing to an insulated pack as Slade plopped her sister next to her.

"Hot chocolate and cookies for *after* we cut the tree."

"But I'm thirsty now."

185

"Then you'll have to wait to cut the tree."

"No!"

"Patience is a virtue, Molly," Slade said as he helped Jamie climb into the front seat, then swung into the rig and settled next to her. With a wink at Jamie, he cracked the whip over the horse's head and the chestnut stepped forward. The sleigh slid easily over the thick snow and through the gates Slade had already opened. Both girls giggled from the back.

"I hadn't planned on this," Jamie said.

"I know." He slid a glance her way, taking in her wool slacks, sweater and overcoat. She wore boots, but they weren't meant for trudging through the snow, nor were her gloves insulated. He placed an arm around her shoulders and, breath fogging in the air, whispered, "Trust me, darlin'. I won't let you freeze." Her breath caught in her lungs for a second, then she looked away, refusing to be seduced by the kind gesture or the care in his voice.

"Here, you drive for a while." He placed the reins in her gloved fingers, then reached beneath the seat and pulled out a sheepskin blanket. As the bells jingled and the sled skimmed across the snow, Slade unfolded the short blanket and tucked it over her lap. As if he cared. Her heart twisted.

He used me, she reminded herself, the old pain returning as she thought of the baby she'd lost, the child she'd mourned alone.

She'd never confided in her grandmother, but Nana had suspected something was wrong. She'd caught Jamie crying behind the barn where Caesar had been grazing, swatting flies with his tail as he nipped at the dry stubble near the fence. Wearing her floppy straw hat and gardening gloves, Nana had rounded the corner with a basket of weeds she'd pulled out of the garden and stopped short when she caught sight of Jamie. "It's that McCafferty boy, isn't it?" she'd guessed, and when Jamie hadn't answered, Nita Parsons had become very serious and placed a gloved hand on Jamie's bare arm. "You would tell me if you needed help, wouldn't you?"

Jamie had nodded and sniffed but hadn't forced the painful words over her tongue.

"Sometimes . . . sometimes a girl gets herself into trouble before she even really thinks about it."

Worried eyes had peered through rimless glasses. "I'm here for you, honey, I always will be, and if that boy has done anything to you, anything at all, I'll take it up with his father. There are laws concerning what can happen between a boy and a girl your age."

"I — I'm fine, Nana," she'd lied, shifting her gaze away from the doubts in her grandmother's eyes.

"You're sure?"

"Absolutely." She'd swallowed back her tears. "I'm just kind of emotional, you know, that time of the month."

Nana's lips had pinched in disbelief, but she hadn't called Jamie on the lie. "Just know that I'm here for you. No matter what." Then she'd dumped her weeds into the growing pile near the barn and walked slowly back to the garden. Jamie had wanted desperately to confide in Nana, but knew it would serve no purpose. Slade had left, was engaged to Sue Ellen, and Jamie had lost the baby. She'd been to see a doctor in a neighboring town who had confirmed the miscarriage. She'd been certain that a part of her had died with her child.

Now, she shivered in the sleigh.

Next to the man who had so callously turned his back on her.

Slade took the reins from her fingers and snapped them. The horse picked up speed across Big Meadow toward the far side where the foothills sloped upward and thick stands of pine and aspen crowded around a creek bed.

In the back seat, the girls giggled and

refused to sit still no matter how many times Slade reminded them to stay put. They were excited, pointing and laughing, chattering about Christmas and Santa and what they wanted.

The horse shied as a rabbit, as white as the snow drifting from the heavens, jumped out of the way and into the safety of skeletal, icy brambles.

"There. That one, that one!" Molly cried, standing quickly and pointing a mittened hand straight ahead, over the horse's ears to a huge tree in the distance.

"I think it's a little big," Slade said, and chuckled to himself as he glanced at the thirty-foot tree. "The General would probably have a heart attack if he had to pull that one back to the house. Then there's me. More than likely, I'd keel over if I had to cut it down. Let's try to find something that will fit *inside* the house."

"Spoilsport," Jamie muttered, caught up in the magic of the moment. He slid her a glance, then clucked to the gelding and snapped the reins. Snowflakes danced and swirled. Frigid air caressed her cheeks.

The acres sped by in a cold, wintry rush as Slade guided General through the foothills until they came to a thick stand of smaller trees. The girls couldn't sit still a moment longer and as Slade reined the horse to a stop, they tumbled out of the sleigh, running pell-mell through the unbroken snow. "I think we'll find one here," he said, climbing out and offering Jamie his arm.

She should ignore it, but looking down into his upturned face, staring into eyes as clear and blue as the summer sky, she grabbed his hand. Something inside her caught. Her heart gave a quick little leap, but she refused to recognize the glimmer in his eyes. She hopped off the sleigh. He tugged on her arm, dragging her close. Before she could so much as catch her breath, he kissed her. Hard. As if he'd been waiting for just the right moment. Chilled lips fastened to hers for an electric instant that caused her heart to kick. Oh, God, her knees turned to water.

The kiss deepened for a second and her blood ran hot. Why was it always like this? Why couldn't she turn away from this one man who seemed determined to break her heart over and over? *Fool me once, shame on you, fool me twice, shame on me . . .*

He lifted his head, then, still holding her, slowly winked at her. "Let's play lumberjack," he suggested, and she arched a brow. He whispered, "I'd prefer doctor, of course, but with the kids around —"

"It wouldn't be proper."

"And you know how dead-set I am about propriety."

She laughed and shook her head as he released her. "You don't give up, do you?"

"Never." He flipped open a compartment in the back of the sleigh and pulled out his tools. Packing a small chain saw in one hand and a coil of nylon rope on his shoulder, he plowed through the snow, following the trails made by tiny little boots.

"Over here! Over here!"

Jamie saw a flash of a pink snowsuit between the saplings.

"Uncle Slade!" Molly was yelling and pointing to a crooked pine tree about ten feet tall. "This one. This one."

"It's not straight, darlin'," he said, eyeing the listing pine.

"It's perfect," Molly insisted, jumping up and down.

"Yeth," her sister said. "This one, Unca Slade."

"She's right, it's . . . perfect," Jamie agreed.

A wry smile twisted Slade's lips. "Out-voted by the females," he mused under his breath. "Well, if you two, er, three, are sure."

"Yeth!" Even Mindy was jumping up and down.

"Cut it down!" Molly demanded.

"Vicious little thing, aren't you? Now, stand back. Both of you." He bent on one knee and looked back at Jamie, who got the message.

"Come on, girls, over here," she said. "Let's give . . . uh, Uncle Slade, some room."

With a growl and plume of smoke, the chain saw roared to life, bucking as the blade bit into the base of the pine. Sawdust plumed and littered the snow. A few seconds later the tree tumbled to the ground, sending up a burst of white powder.

The girls sprang forward. Insisting upon helping their uncle, they unlooped the coil of rope as he baled the tree.

"Good job," he said, carrying the tree back to the sleigh and tying it to one side, above the runners. "I'll recommend you both to the Lumberjack Hall of Fame."

"Can we gets another one?" Molly asked, her eyes bright as she spied another tree.

"I think one's enough, sprite." He rubbed the top of her head and she grinned widely. "We'll take this one back and maybe make some snow angels or a snowman while the tree dries out, then we'll take it inside and you can get your aunt Randi to help you decorate it."

Mindy's mittened hands clasped together at the thought. "With candy canes?"

"If that's what you want." Slade tested the ropes lashing the tree to the sleigh. The bundled pine didn't move. "Okay, how about cookies and cocoa?"

They ate in the sleigh, the twins chattering in the still afternoon air, the warm smells of hot chocolate and coffee drifting through the snowflakes that swirled around them. It felt so natural, so right, with thick blankets and sheepskin tossed over their laps, noses red with the cold, laughter coming easy. As if they were a family, Jamie thought. The family she'd never really known.

Except that the children weren't hers.

Except that she wasn't married to Slade.

Except that he'd left her years ago.

Except that the baby they'd created hadn't survived long enough to be born.

Hot tears burned the backs of her eyes and Slade reached forward to touch her cheek. "Somethin' wrong?"

If you only knew, she thought, but shook her head. "Nah. Just a little nostalgia."

"For?"

"Things that could have been." That was vague enough. She sipped her coffee and felt its heat burn a path down her throat.

But it couldn't warm that icy spot in her heart, the part that had died when Slade had left her and she'd lost their child.

"Maybe you should start lookin' forward, instead of lookin' back," he suggested, as if he could read her mind.

"You're a great one to give that kind of advice." She'd seen the torment in his expression when he'd mentioned the accident that had taken the life of someone close to him. It was her turn to touch, the finger of one kidskin glove tracing his scar. "You still beat yourself up for this."

His expression changed. Darkened. As if the demons he'd so recently put to rest had awakened. His lips pursed for a second and he tossed the dregs from his cup into the snow. "I don't think we should go there."

"You said —"

"Go where?" Molly asked, leaning forward, breaking into the tense conversation. "Where should we go?"

"Never mind." Slade half turned in the seat. "Let's pack up our things and head back before it gets dark. Hiya!" He slapped the reins over General's rump and the sleigh eased forward.

Twisting over the seat back, Jamie wiped smudged faces and tucked the two uneaten cookies and empty cups into the insulated pack, then settled into the front seat as the girls snuggled under their blankets.

Slade stared straight ahead, his jaw set, pain etching his features as darkness crept through the trees and into the gullies. Rudders gliding, the sleigh slid over the smooth snow. Snowflakes swirled and caught in Jamie's hair and eyelashes as the words to "Winter Wonderland" rolled through her mind. She cast a glance at Slade, his lips compressed. Dear God, how she'd loved him all those years ago. If things had been different, perhaps they would have . . .

Stop it! What would have been better? That he found out you were pregnant and married you because he felt obligated? That you gave up your dreams of college and career to be what? Slade McCafferty's wife? That's not what you wanted.

No, Jamie thought as the night closed in around them. But the baby, oh, how she'd wanted the baby. And there was more. Whether she wanted to admit it or not, she'd wanted Slade to love her.

CHAPTER TEN

"Did you see that?" Slade's eyes narrowed on the stables. He reined General to a stop near the front porch of the ranch house. Was it his imagination, or had he seen someone's face in the darkened window of the horse barn?

"What?" Jamie asked.

"Someone inside the stables . . . not Larry Todd, our foreman, or Adam Zollander, our ranch hand, or one of my brothers." His voice sounded tight, even to his own ears, and every muscle in his body tensed. He dropped the reins as Jamie swung her head, surveying the outbuildings surrounding the yard.

"I don't see anyone," she said.

"Neither do I. Now." But he had.

Or was he just jumping at shadows? Edgy because of the attempts on Randi's life? He wasn't willing to take any chances, and the gut feeling he had — that something wasn't right — stuck with him. "You take the kids inside. I'll go check it out." He was out of the sleigh in an instant.

"What about the tree?" Molly demanded as she flung herself into a thick, soft, drift.

"I'll get it later."

"But —"

He focused hard on his niece. "I said I'll bring it in. Later. Or you can have Uncle Matt or Thorne do it now. But you two —" he motioned to both of his nieces "— go inside and warm up."

"I wants to do snow angels!" Molly was as stubborn as he was, but this wasn't the time to back down, not when the hairs on the back of his neck were rising. He glanced at Jamie, sending her a silent message that she picked up.

"Come on, girls," Jamie said, ushering both rambunctious twins toward the front door. "Maybe Juanita has something for you in the kitchen."

"Dumb Buandita," Molly muttered, but as Mindy climbed onto the first step, the door swept open and the twins shrieked in glee at the sight of their mother.

"Mommy, Mommy, we gots the tree! Look! Uncle Slade, he sawed it down —" Mindy was pointing frantically at the sleigh, but Slade ignored the little girl and, jabbing

197

his fists into the pockets of his jacket, trudged through the snow to the stables. He considered a weapon, but figured he'd grab a pitchfork once he was inside the barn.

It's probably nothing, his mind nagged. But he wasn't willing to take a chance. Not on his sister's life. Not on the baby's. Not on anyone in his family's. And not on Jamie's. He stopped short. Jamie wasn't part of his family.

Whoa.

He was getting ahead of himself. Way ahead. He made it to the barn door, swung it open and reached inside, but didn't flip the switch. If someone was lurking in the shadows with a gun, he didn't want to give the guy an open shot at him.

Instead, he grabbed a pitchfork as he slipped inside. Horses snorted and shifted in their stalls. One gave out a nervous nicker as Slade waited in the darkness, ears straining, listening for the slightest noise. His fingers grasped the smooth wooden handle of the pitchfork and he crouched, keeping his back to the wall. Did he hear the scrape of a boot or was his mind playing tricks on him? Was there a change in the atmosphere inside the old building or was he jumping at shadows?

His eyes adjusted to the blue light shining

through the windows, a watery illumination from the exterior security lamps. Slade made out the familiar shapes of the horses as they dozed in their stalls. Nothing appeared out of place. Silently he crept along the walk between the stalls, his pitchfork ready. He peeked cautiously into each box, expecting a figure to leap out of the shadows at any second. A few of the horses snorted. One pawed the straw, and despite the chill in the air, Slade felt a trickle of nervous sweat slide down his spine.

Did he smell something . . . the hint of some aftershave still hanging on the air, or was he, again, conjuring up a sinister scenario that didn't exist?

A mouse scurried across the floor and he jumped, landing on the balls of his feet. But there was nothing but the sound of frantic little claws on concrete.

Slade paused at Diablo Rojo's stall, the very end box. The colt tossed his head and huffed out a disgusted blast of air, as if he knew the folly of it all.

Silently, Slade slipped around the last box to the next aisle and as he walked between the set of stalls, he saw no one. Heard nothing out of place. Maybe he'd imagined the face in the window. Unconvinced, he searched the tack room, again, without bothering with the lights. Nothing seemed out of place. He stepped on the lowest rung of the ladder to the hayloft.

The door burst open. Slade spun, his weapon ready. The lights blazed on.

"What the devil's got into you?" Matt stood in the doorway, his eyes focused on the sharp tines of the pitchfork aimed in his direction.

The knots in Slade's shoulders relaxed a little. "I thought I saw someone here when I brought the twins back to the house."

"So what . . . you thought you'd surprise him and prong him to death? Like somethin' you were going to put on the barbecue? Hell, why didn't you grab Dad's rifle?"

"I wasn't sure."

"But you thought you'd grab the pitchfork just in case."

"Yeah."

"Damn." Matt's smile twisted in open amusement. "Sometimes I don't know what the hell you're thinkin'." Matt walked to a shelf where a pair of leather gloves was tucked between the curry combs and brushes. "Seems to me you've been jumping out of your skin ever since a certain lady lawyer showed up in town." He picked up the gloves and pulled them on.

"Meaning?"

"Meaning anything you want it to." Chuckling under his breath, Matt headed for the door. "I guess I'll leave you and the bogeyman alone. But I will haul the Christmas tree into the house. The girls can't wait."

"Do that," Slade growled irritably.

"Then I'll put the sleigh away and take care of General."

"Thanks."

"No problem." Still chuckling to himself, Matt yanked on the gloves and disappeared through the door. Slade felt like a fool. But he couldn't shake the feeling that something was wrong, so, with the interior lights burning bright, he climbed the ladder to the hayloft where the air barely moved. The smells of hay and horses, dust and dung filtered upward. The lights were dimmer here, the shadows murkier. Bales were stacked to the high, pitched ceiling and loose straw was several inches thick across the old plank floor. But there wasn't a sound up here. Nothing looked out of place. Nothing moved.

Fool. You're starting to be paranoid.

Downstairs, the door creaked open.

Slade nearly jumped out of his skin.

"Slade?"

Jamie's voice. He relaxed a little.

"Up here." Looking down the ladder, he found her craning her neck and staring up at the hole cut into the floor.

"Find anything?"

"Just Matt. And that was pretty scary."

She smiled and shook her head. "You can be funny when you're not a pain in the backside."

"I'll take that as a compliment, Counselor. Come on up."

She hesitated. Frowned enough to create little furrows between her eyebrows. "What about the twins? They're waiting for you. When it comes to promises about Christmas trees and snow angels, kids have incredible memories."

"They can wait a little longer. It's the anticipation that's the fun part." He crooked a finger at her. "Come on up."

"Well, I don't think I should —"

"Afraid?"

"What? Afraid? Of you?" Her eyes sparked. She couldn't resist a dare.

"Of us."

"I told you —"

"Yeah, yeah, I know." God she was beautiful. Staring up at him with wide hazel eyes filled with indecision. "Come on, Jamie, it's time to drop the sword. I won't hurt you. I don't bite . . . well, not hard and only if the lady asks for —"

"Oh, save it, McCafferty." He saw it then, that little shadow of pain that he'd witnessed before, but she quickly disguised it with a determined thrust of her chin. She grabbed the metal rung and stepped onto the ladder. Within seconds she was up in the hayloft, looking out of place in her wool slacks, sweater and overcoat.

"Sit," he suggested, kicking a bale toward her.

"You've got something you want to say," she guessed, smoothing her coat before perching on the edge of the bale.

"Yeah. I do." He sat next to her, his hands clasped between his knees. "I enjoyed myself this afternoon."

Worry clouded her eyes. "Oh."

"Didn't you?"

"Well, yes. The girls were so excited, and it's been years since I was out in the wilderness to cut a tree. I usually get a small one from a lot in town."

"That wasn't what I was talking about, and you know it."

She glanced up at him, then let her gaze slide away as if she were suddenly interested in the rafters and the feathers and droppings from an owl that had once roosted near the small round window high above.

The barest hint of her perfume tickled his nostrils, and he couldn't help but notice the slope of her cheek and the way her lips folded in on themselves.

"I was talking about being with you," he admitted when she didn't say a word. "Yes, I know it sounds corny."

"Like a line out of a sappy romantic movie," she said, but her voice had changed, deepened.

"Yeah, maybe." He snorted a laugh, his fingers laced with hers. "But I meant it." He tipped her chin up with one gloved finger, gazed into her incredible eyes for just a second, then pressed his lips to hers. She uttered the tiniest moan of protest, then sighed against him. His blood heated. He wrapped one arm around her, pushing closer, feeling her mouth part slightly as his tongue touched the sexy seam of her lips.

Don't do this, his mind screamed. But he didn't listen. Wouldn't. He'd spent the past week waking up in the middle of the night so hard he couldn't think straight, drenched in sweat from the vivid dreams he'd had of kissing her, touching her, making love to her, and now they were alone and he felt the heat throb between them, the passion she denied just beneath the surface. He pressed harder, his tongue sliding along the slick ridges of the roof of her mouth, her tongue playing with his, her breathing shallow. Rapid. Warm. "Slade," she whispered as he pulled back to look at her flushed face and to smooth a lock of hair from her cheek.

"What, darlin'?"

"This isn't a good idea."

"You got that right."

"I mean . . . I think it's a bad idea."

"Probably."

"We're going to regret this."

"Never." He nuzzled her cheek and she quivered, her fingers tracing the slopes of his shoulders. Horses moved and nickered beneath them and in the muted light Slade worked at the buttons of her coat, pressed her down until they tumbled off the bale onto the loose hay.

"Please, listen . . ." She looked up at him and he was lost in that troubled hazel gaze.

He levered himself on one elbow. "I'm listening."

"This . . . you and me . . . it's dangerous . . . we'd better leave it alone."

"Because of the other guy."

" 'Other guy'?" she repeated, and those two sexy little lines appeared between her eyebrows again.

"Your boss."

"Oh. Chuck."

"Yeah. Chuck." The guy's name even tasted bad.

"It's not about Chuck," she admitted honestly as he plucked a piece of straw from her hair.

"Well, to tell the truth, I don't give a damn. Right now, Jamie, it's just you and me," he said, and kissed her again, his mouth slanting over hers as a wave of possession washed over him. He didn't want to talk about the past or her boyfriend or anything else. They were here. Together. Alone. A man and woman. He wanted her. More than he'd wanted a woman in a long, long time. For the first time since Rebecca . . . squeezing his eyes shut, he concentrated on Jamie. The touch and feel of her. Old memories reawakened, long-forgotten emotions surfaced. He heard her sigh, felt the sweet pressure of her lips on his, sensed her shift from denial to need.

His jeans were suddenly too restricting, the thickness in his crotch beginning to ache as he tossed off his jacket. He stretched out over her, unbuttoned her coat and reached beneath the hem of her sweater. Her skin was warm and smooth to his touch. She gasped as his hands scaled her ribs to dip inside her bra.

"I don't . . . I don't know . . ."

"Shh," he breathed into her mouth, kissing her, his tongue mating with hers as he stroked her breast.

"Oo-oh," she moaned as the tip of his finger scraped her nipple. She bucked beneath him, held on tight, kissed him back. Her fingers dug into his shoulders as he kissed the side of her neck, then, lifting the sweater over her head, pressed urgent lips to that warm, dusky hollow of her throat. Her pulse jumped beneath the ministrations of his tongue and her fingernails dug deep into his muscles.

Slowly he lowered himself, kissing the tops of her breasts, touching the lacy edge of her bra with his tongue. Her fingers curled in his hair and she guided him to one nipple. Gently he lifted the breast from its bonds and tentatively tasted of her, his tongue tickling the very tip of her nipple, his lips just brushing that puckering little bud.

"Slade," she moaned insistently, pulling his head closer.

"Oh, darlin', there's no need to rush," he breathed across her wet skin. But she was ready. Hot. Anxious. He saw it in her eyes. She wanted him, damn it.

He slipped a hand beneath the waistband of her slacks and she sucked in her stomach and began working at the buttons of his shirt. "You want me," he said, and she didn't answer. "Come on, Counselor, admit it."

"*You* want *me*," she said, telling herself that she was about to make a mistake of epic proportions.

"Oh, baby, yes." He unbuttoned her slacks, pulled them down over her hips and kissed his way along her abdomen. His tongue was moist and warm in the cold air. Tantalizing. Tempting.

She told herself she couldn't do this, not again. Yet the words of denial slipped away from her as he slowly slid her panty hose down her legs, the tips of his fingers tickling her, his lips following the same sensual path.

No! No! No! What was she thinking? This was a mistake of epic proportions. His hands were kneading her buttocks and the stubble of his beard grazed the skin of her inner thighs. She wiggled. He held her fast. Hot fingers dug into her flesh. Warm breath steamed against her skin. Inside she throbbed, felt moist. Wet. His lips and tongue skimmed closer.

Skilled hands massaged her hips.

This is so dangerous . . . a big mistake . . . remember how he hurt you, her mind screamed from some distant, far-off shore. But her bones were melting, her breathing difficult, and her entire being seemed to center where he touched her, at that private place where her legs joined. They parted of their own accord.

"That's a girl," he said as she arched upward and felt air from his lungs whisper over the curls down below. "Let me in, Jamie."

She wriggled, desire beating through her, need burning in her blood. She closed her eyes, felt the warmth of her coat beneath her and the cool air above. And Slade, she felt Slade kiss her, his lips caressing her so gently tears burned behind her eyelids and her throat caught. She couldn't stop, didn't want to. She craved more of him. She thought she'd go mad with his slow, deliberate ministrations. "Slade," she cried, lifting her eager hips to meet him, arching as she felt the slick penetration of his tongue.

"Oh," she cried, her fingers curling in the loose straw. "Oh, oh, oooooohhhh." She shuddered, her eyes opening to see the timbers of the hayloft swirl above her. The hayloft spun and she convulsed, sweat running down her body.

Then he was upon her, kicking off his jeans, stretching his long, lean body against hers, rubbing his flesh against her fevered skin. He kissed her hard. With purpose. His hands were no longer gentle, but firm as they kneaded her flesh. He pressed his hungry mouth to hers and kissed her as if he would never stop.

Her arms wound around his neck. She felt his hard, sinewy muscles as she kissed him wildly. Madly.

She threw all her inhibitions to the raw Montana wind. This is all that mattered. Here. Now. Slade McCafferty.

"You're so incredible," he breathed, voice raspy, face flushed. He prodded her legs apart, used his hands to lift her buttocks and, thrusting hard, stared straight into her eyes. She gasped.

He slid out, then drove forward again.

"Oh . . . Slade . . ."

Again.

She clung to him, her neck bowed as she met each hard stroke. Again and again, faster and faster, until the center of the universe seemed to spin within that sensual spot where their bodies joined, until she could think of nothing but the pure animal pleasure of his body melding with hers, until sweat drizzled down their fused bodies despite the cold winter air. He kissed her. Hard. Desperately.

"Jamie," he whispered in a rush. "Jamie, oh . . . woman . . . Oh . . ."

She spasmed. Cried out. The stables whirled around them, the sound of horses far off as he collapsed against her, breathing hard, his body dripping with sweat, his arms surrounding her.

Tears threatened her eyes as he held her. How many times had she thought of making love to him, of feeling his hard body pressed against hers, or kissing him until her lips were raw? It had been her dream, long ago, one she'd tried determinedly to forget.

And here she was. In the hayloft of the Flying M ranch, feeling Slade's warm breath ruffle her hair and knowing she'd probably made the second worst mistake of her life. The first had been falling in love with him all those years ago.

Oh, what had she done?

She blinked hard. She wouldn't break down. No . . . what was done, was done . . . she would have to live with it.

He levered himself up on one elbow and, grinning widely, looked down at her. "Well, well, well."

"My thoughts exactly," she lied, trying to slide away from him, embarrassment coloring her cheeks. "I . . . I don't know what got into me —"

"I do."

"I wasn't talking about *that*."

"Neither was I."

"Right. Look, this has been fun and all —" Oh, dear, listen to her ramble on. "But I really should be going."

His blue eyes gleamed wickedly. "So soon?"

"You know my motto — 'Love 'em and leave 'em.' Oh, no, wait, that was yours." She regretted the words the second they tripped over her tongue.

His eyes darkened. His smile disappeared. "I tried to explain —"

"And I wouldn't let you." She held up a hand and reached for her panties. "I know."

"That's right. You wouldn't." Quickly he lunged, his hands grabbing her wrists, his weight pinning her down.

"Okay, okay, I give," she said, regretting the bad joke. "I made a mistake."

"No. I did. When I left you."

Her throat thickened. A lump formed. Oh, for the love of Pete, she couldn't break down. Not now. Not after all the years of bearing the pain alone. "You don't have to —"

"I know I don't. I'm just tellin' you what I feel. Isn't that what women always complain about men? That they aren't in touch with their feelings? That they never say what's on their mind? Well, I'm tellin' you. I made a mistake. I didn't know it at the time. Hell, I didn't know it for years. But I know it now, okay?" Intense eyes stared down at her and not a trace of the amusement she'd seen in his expression only seconds before lingered. "Jamie, do you hear me?"

"Yes." She couldn't breathe. Her eyes filled and she blinked hard. This couldn't be happening. She thought of the summer they'd been together, the lovemaking . . . their baby.

"What?"

"It's . . . it's nothing."

"The hell it is." He released one wrist and wiped a tear that had begun to drizzle from her eye.

"Damn."

"What's this all about?" he demanded, glaring at her. "You're holding back."

"It doesn't matter." She brushed the tears quickly aside with her free hand.

"It sure as hell matters to you."

"It was a long time ago."

His eyes narrowed thoughtfully as he stared down at her and she bit her lower lip, refusing to break down. "What is it? There's something else, isn't there? Something I don't know about."

She tried to wriggle free, but his hands

were like manacles, his weight immovable.

"What?"

Why not tell him the truth? Let him deal with it?

Because it would serve no purpose. Only open old wounds.

"Come on, there's something, Counselor, some deep dark secret that you're hiding from me."

Taking a deep breath, certain that her voice would fail her, she braced herself. "All right," she finally acquiesced. "If you want to know the truth, it's pretty simple. When you left me, I was pregnant."

"What?" The color seeped from his face in one instant. He released her wrists. "Pregnant?" he repeated in a hoarse whisper.

"That's right."

"But the baby? Where is . . ."

In for a penny, in for a pound. There was no turning back now. "I miscarried, Slade. Right off the bat. One month it was confirmed I was pregnant, the next . . ." Her throat closed and she felt another tear slide down her face before she was able to pull herself together. "The next month . . . I wasn't."

"Why?" His eyes were dark as the night.

"I don't know," she said, then saw the

214

hardness of his jaw, the anger in the lines of his face. "Don't you even suggest that it was anything other than natural," she said, reading the unspoken message in his gaze, "because that's just what happened, okay? And it really isn't any of your business."

"My child isn't my business?"

"You were already gone, remember? You'd walked out on me and so it wasn't your concern. Did you ever call? Ever stop by? Ever write?" she challenged, her chin trembling as he rolled off her and stared in disbelief. She scooped up her clothes and started struggling into them, her fingernails ripping through her panty hose in her haste. "No. You didn't. Why? Because you didn't give a damn."

"That's not how it was." But his words lacked conviction, and her stupid heart tore again.

"No?" She yanked her slacks over her hips. "Then tell me, how was it? Hmm? Because from where I sat, alone, pregnant, not knowing what to do, it sure felt like you left me for another woman."

His face flushed a deep, angry scarlet as he reached for his clothes. "If you had told me —"

"About the baby? Would that have made a difference in how you felt? Is that what you're trying to say? I wasn't good enough, but, gee, if I had your baby, then suddenly I was?" she stormed, tossing on her sweater and stuffing her arms angrily down the sleeves.

Slade had pulled on his jeans as she reached for her coat. "I made a mistake."

"That makes two of us, and now . . . now we've made another, but let's just forget it, okay? We've literally had our roll in the hay, and now we can go back to our normal, regular lives." She cast a glance down at the mussed straw, then rolled her eyes at her own stupidity and marched to the ladder. She was down the rungs and out the door of the stables in less than a minute.

The cold air hit her with the force of a northern gale. What was she thinking, confiding in Slade? She'd read the accusations in his eyes. Damn it all, she should never have told him. Never.

She strode through the snow as best she could, made her way to the car, reached for the handle and realized her purse and briefcase were at the house. Well, fine. Turning on her heel she started for the snow-covered walk. In the living room window stood the Christmas tree. The two little girls were dancing around it, holding up tinsel and glittering decorations, laughing and giggling as Nicole and Randi strung lights around the branches. Through the panes, she saw Thorne. His face was relaxed, a wide, adoring smile on his face as he gazed at his wife.

Jamie's heart shattered into a million pieces. The scene through the frosted windowpanes was something right out of Currier and Ives, everything she'd once hoped for, everything she'd thought, naively, that she might have with Slade and their child . . . She bit her lip, fought tears. From the corner of her eye she saw Matt walking General to the stables. He and Kelly were about to be married, to increase the McCafferty family.

Jamie had to leave. Now. She couldn't take another minute of this perfect family holiday scene.

Slade burst out of the stables. Furious eyes focused on Jamie, he hitched his way through the drifts. Great. Just what she didn't need. She couldn't face another showdown, not now. She was too raw.

She started for the house.

"Jamie! Wait!"

No way in hell.

She marched up the steps to the front door and without knocking and disturbing the decorating party, eased into the front hallway. Music and the smells of apples and cinnamon greeted her. Burl Ives was singing some lighthearted Christmas carol from the CD player and the twins' high-pitched voices chirped above the song.

"I want to puts it on," one little voice insisted on the other side of the wall in the living room.

"You can, honey, just let me get the lights in place." Nicole seemed always the voice of reason.

Thorne said, "That's right . . . here ya go. Why don't you try the switch, now, then put the ornament on? Here let me get the main lights."

Jamie thought of the baby she'd lost and fought tears. She slung the strap of her purse over her shoulder and reached for her briefcase. She cast a final glance to the archway separating the landing at the base of the stairs and the living room.

"Okay, now," Thorne said as the house lights dimmed.

"O-hhh," one of the girls said.

"Ith's be-you-ti-ful," the other agreed, and Jamie saw the reflection of colored Christmas lights on the wall. They'd turned on the tree.

Jamie couldn't listen a minute longer.

Armed with her briefcase, she turned.

The door burst open.

Slade McCafferty, all six feet of glorious anger, filled the door frame.

"Excuse me," she said, trying to dodge past him.

"Not yet." He grabbed her arm roughly and she sent him a glare as icy as the day.

"Let go of me, McCafferty," she warned as the sound of a car, tires spinning in the snow, engine purring, reached her ears.

"Now what?" Slade looked over his shoulder, and Jamie caught a glimpse of the new visitor as he climbed out of his silver Mercedes. Her heart nose-dived as she recognized the driver.

Chuck Jansen had arrived.

CHAPTER ELEVEN

"I thought I might find you here." Chuck's affable grin was wide as he walked up the steps to the front porch where Jamie and Slade were standing. Tall, lean, tanned from skiing in the winter and golf in the summer, Chuck leaned forward to hug Jamie, but stopped short. His smile faded, and the arms that he'd opened fell to his side when he saw Slade's hand upon the sleeve of her coat.

"I was just leaving," she said awkwardly. Of all the times for him to show up. She yanked her arm away from Slade's hand. "Chuck Jansen, this is Slade McCafferty."

Eyeing each other warily, the two men shook hands as Randi, holding her sleeping baby to her shoulder, stepped into the foyer through the archway from the living room. "I thought I felt a draft. For Pete's sake, Slade, close the door —" Her expression changed from mild irritation to concern, her eyebrows pulling together, her arms inadvertently tightening over her child as she saw the stranger.

"Randi, I'd like you to meet my boss and a senior partner for Jansen, Monteith and Stone," Jamie said, recovering quickly as Slade pulled the door shut and little Joshua Ray let out a soft, sleepy gurgle.

More introductions were made as they eased into the living room, and Jamie realized her escape from the Flying M would have to be delayed.

"Chuck!" Thorne, looping a strand of tiny gold beads over the tree's sagging branches, peered through the uneven boughs as Randi carried her son upstairs.

The attorney grinned. "I never thought I'd see the day," Chuck observed as the twins clustered glittering ornaments on the lower branches.

Nicole, after a quick "Nice to meet you" and perfunctory handshake, continued sorting through dozens of boxes of decorations.

Jamie wanted to vaporize.

Chuck had recovered from the shock of seeing Jamie with another man. "I just didn't think domesticity was ever your thing," he said, needling Thorne.

"I'm a changed person these days." Thorne cast a loving glance at his wife and stepdaughters. "A family man."

"I see." Was there amusement in Chuck's voice, or just disbelief? As if a McCafferty could never settle down.

"Let me get your coat," Nicole suggested, and Jamie, wishing she were anyplace else on earth, suffered through the small talk and offer of refreshments, all the while aware of Slade's gaze upon her.

She realized that tiny pieces of straw were sticking to her coat and that her hair was a mess, probably punctuated with hay, as well, her clothes askew. She just wanted to leave, but Chuck had different plans and had her sit in as he asked for an update on the transfer of the property. He and Thorne cradled drinks and traded stories about practicing law together for a brief but obviously memorable time, then they moved to the dining room table and a pot of coffee.

Jamie felt like the underling she was. Worse yet, she sensed that Chuck was making a point about who was in charge of the McCaffertys as clients. Chuck and Thorne had worked together, and the intimation was that they were part of the same "good ol' boys club," an idea as antiquated as some of the furniture that still graced the law offices at Jansen, Monteith and Stone.

Jamie didn't make too many waves, but

did explain what was happening with the deed transfer and sale of the acreage. She didn't mention calling Felicia Reynolds about the baby's custody, nor did she bring up Thorne wanting the firm to use any means possible to locate Joshua's father. Chuck was in error on a couple of points concerning the title transfer, and Jamie gently straightened him out. She wondered about that. Chuck was pretty sharp. Was he testing her?

While sipping coffee, they discussed every aspect of current legal concerns, and Chuck, good-naturedly, pitched the firm again, suggesting that "J.M.S.," as he liked to refer to the law firm, could do a lot more for Thorne and his siblings.

It was after seven by the time Jamie left. Chuck promised to stop by her place. He suggested they go to dinner so that he could catch up on all she'd been up to. Slade, seated insolently across the table from Jamie, had listened to the exchange silently. He'd kicked out his chair and rested on the small of his back as he witnessed the interplay between Jamie, Chuck and Thorne, but he hadn't said a word.

It was the longest hour of Jamie's life. When Thorne offered drinks and cigars, Chuck accepted, and she made a quick excuse of having to get back to her house. No one argued, least of all Slade. She made her way to her car and was surprised when she heard footsteps behind her.

"You're not seriously considering marrying that pompous ass, are you?" Slade asked, and Jamie gnashed her teeth as she opened the car door and turned to face him. Snow was falling again, creating a soft, shifting curtain between the parking area and the house where the windows glowed warmly, yellow patches of light in the coming night.

"I was thinking about it, yes," she admitted.

Slade's face was serious. "You'd be bored inside of a month."

"You don't know Chuck."

"That's right. And I'm not sure I want to. That guy's dry as a bone on a desert carcass."

"Thanks for the advice," she said sarcastically. "I'll keep it in mind."

"Do."

She tossed her briefcase onto the passenger seat.

"There's something else you should keep in mind, as well."

"Oh? What's that?" she asked, turning as his arms surrounded her and he pinned her to the car. "Now, wait a second."

"Nope." His lips crashed down on hers, reminding her of their recent lovemaking. He kissed her hard. Long. To the point that her knees threatened to give way and her heart pounded a thousand times a minute. The memory of making love with him was fresh, the scent of his skin tantalizing . . . Why did she feel this way about him? Why? Chemistry? Forbidden fruit? Flirting with the devil?

Or was she just plain nuts? A masochist who wanted her heart broken a dozen times over?

Slade lifted his head and looked at her with smoky-blue eyes. "That, Jamie. That's what I want you to keep in mind," he said as he released her and started for the stables in his long, easy stride. Breathless, she slumped against the car. Then she smelled a trace of cigar smoke and noticed three men on the front porch. Thorne and Matt McCafferty were cradling drinks, smoking big cigars and talking with Chuck Jansen.

"Wonderful," she muttered under her breath as she slid behind the wheel and twisted her key in the ignition. Her little car sparked to life. She rammed it into reverse and caught a glimpse of Slade in the rearview mirror. She threw the compact into first. With a spray of snow she was heading down the long lane of Flying M and wondering how in the world she was going to break it off with her boss.

". . . so you and Slade McCafferty," Chuck said as they sat across the table in a booth at a small restaurant in Grand Hope.

They'd spent the meal talking about what was going on at the office, how the repairs to Jamie's grandmother's house were coming along and the legal work the firm was handling for the McCaffertys, including discussion of Randi's baby, custody rights and the identity of the missing father. But the conversation had steered clear of her involvement with Slade. Until now.

"Slade and I have a history." She pushed her plate aside, half her fillet untouched.

"Do you? You never mentioned it."

"Didn't see the need."

A slim, blond waitress swept by and cleared off the plates. Bland music drifted around the cavernous room split by half walls and booths.

"So what're you going to do about it? A history is one thing, a future another." Chuck reached across the table and took her hand in his. "You know how I feel about you, Jamie. I was hoping you and I could work things out." Gently he stroked the backs of her knuckles with the pad of his thumb.

"I don't think that will happen," she said, and withdrew her hand. "We want different things."

"And you and McCafferty don't?"

"This isn't about Slade," she insisted, holding his gaze. "It's about you and me."

"I love you."

She shook her head. "But you ridicule me."

"No, I —"

"Sure you do, Chuck. You did so a couple of hours ago with that tired old song and dance with Thorne at the Flying M. You tried to show me up, all under the guise of being my boss, of caring for me, of mentoring me, when we both know you did it because I'm a woman."

"What?" His face showed sincere shock. "What the devil are you talking about?"

"You should have backed me up, Chuck. Instead, you tried to show me up by pointing out where I could have made a mistake, and you were grinning while you were doing it. That was the worst part. As if Thorne and you were in on some private joke over the poor dumb woman."

"That's ridiculous, Jamie. Paranoid. I

never hire by race or creed or sex, you know that."

Jamie barreled on. "The point you were trying to make was that, 'Hey, I've got this young woman handling the case and she's pretty good, but you know —' and this is where you wanted to insert a wink, wink, just to make sure that Thorne was on the same wavelength '— she's just a pretty underling.'"

"I didn't do anything of the sort!"

"Sure you did. If Frank Kepler or Morty Freeman or Scott Chavez had been in the room and you'd thought they'd made a mistake, you would have taken a firm line with them, pointed to the error and cleared it up one way or another. There wouldn't have been any of this patronizing, I'm-such-a-good-guy-helping-out-this-poor-little-woman attitude."

"I didn't."

"Hogwash. I was there, Chuck." She hooked her thumb at her chest. "And it made me feel small."

He was actually horrified. Didn't believe a word she was telling him. "Maybe you were overly sensitive. Maybe you were trying to make a big splash, impress the McCafferty brothers. Especially the hellion."

"Low blow, Chuck."

"But true."

She couldn't argue that point. Because some of his argument was true. There was a part of her, a small, petty part, that wanted to rub Slade's nose in the fact that she'd grown into a successful attorney, that she'd become the kind of woman good enough for him, the kind of woman he'd thrown her over for years ago. She had money, looks, charm and success.

So what?

Big deal.

Right now it seemed trivial and vain. She poured cream into her coffee. Chuck was smart, was used to reading human emotion for the witness stand, so he probably understood the emotions she tried vainly to hide. Her need to prove herself to Slade was just wounded pride talking. Deep down, she knew that dealing with Slade was only asking — no, make that *begging* — for trouble. The kind of trouble she didn't need.

And yet you made love to him. Wild, crazy, cast-all-your-worries-to-the-wind love. You haven't gotten over him. All those years and all the pain, and you're still a foolish, lonely girl who finds him sexy as hell. Which is just plain stupid.

His devil-may-care attitude may have matured a bit, but he's still a wild man, one who isn't putting down any roots, one to whom home is the open highway. And that's not what you want. Or is it?

She took a sip from her cup, then set it down and stared at Chuck. "Regardless of what I do or don't feel for Slade McCafferty, it's not working for us. You and me. It hasn't been for a long time and we both know it."

A silver eyebrow lifted, begging her to continue.

"We want different things in life, Chuck. We're at different places in our lives."

"And I'm a supercilious prick."

She nearly choked on a swallow of coffee, then dabbed at her lips with a napkin and nodded. "Well . . . yeah . . . sometimes."

"Maybe I need a strong woman to keep me in line."

"Definitely. But not me."

Sighing, he folded his arms across his chest and leaned back against the booth. "I guess you don't realize how much I love you and, yes, how much I like you. And that's important. Whether you know it or not. You've never been married. Sure the passion, the spark, is important, but you've got to be compatible with the person you choose. You've got to like him."

She didn't disagree.

"And you're right in the respect that I don't want to have more children. Three is enough, if not just financially, then emotionally, personally and globally, as well. I've already done my share of leaving my genetic imprint, if you will, and, also, I've suffered through diaper changing, scraped knees, broken hearts and car wrecks — none of which is easy, all of which, I know, is important.

"But now I'm paying through the nose for college. By the time the last one is finished — and this isn't including grad school — I'll be almost ready to retire. I'm just not willing to start over and do it again. I want some time for me. What's left over I need to give to the kids I've already got and the grandkids that will inevitably come along. My children deserve that."

"And what about your new wife? Would she get any of that precious time of yours?"

"That goes without saying."

"Does it?" She shook her head. It wasn't that she didn't believe him. Chuck was baring his soul; she knew that. But it still wouldn't work. Not for them. "I can't give up the dream, Chuck. I won't. Call me old-fashioned, or even a dreamer, but I want it all — a career, a husband, babies, station wagon — no, make that a minivan — and a cute little house with a garden, swing set and white picket fence."

"And you think Slade McCafferty can give you those things?"

"I doubt it. I'm not talking about Slade or what he wants. I'm talking about me." She opened her purse, withdrew her wallet and flipped it open.

"What are you doing?" He was aghast.

"Paying for my dinner." She slid out her credit card.

"No way. This is on me. On J.M.S." He was already reaching into his jacket pocket.

"Not this time."

"I insist."

"Of course you do." She caught the waitress's eye. "Would you ring this up for me?" she asked when the girl stepped to the table.

"Bring me the bill," Chuck ordered the blonde.

"I —"

"I don't want to hear another word about it."

Jamie's temper flared. "That's just what I'm talking about."

"I asked you to dinner."

"Should I split the bill?" the waitress, her face anxious, offered.

"No!" Chuck was adamant, his male pride shredded.

232

"No, I'll get it." Jamie slapped her card into the startled woman's hand and she glared directly at her boss. "And I don't want to hear another word about it."

"This is ridiculous," Chuck snapped. "Beyond ridiculous."

They waited in tense silence. When the waitress returned, Jamie added a healthy tip to the tab and signed her name to the receipt. She felt freer than she had in years.

On the other hand, Chuck stewed. He tried not to be churlish, but he was steamed. Deep furrows lined his brow.

As the waitress turned her attention to another booth, Jamie hauled her purse from the bench beside her.

"You can expense out the meal," Chuck finally said, as if he was trying to find some way to deal with her erratic behavior.

"I know I can, but I won't." Jamie stood and looked down at the man she had nearly married. Oh, God, what a mistake that would have been. Impulsively she added, "I quit, Chuck. Not just this relationship, but the firm, as well."

"Wait a minute, Jamie. Quit? No. *Now* you're acting like an emotional female."

"Well, good. Because that's what I am. But I'm also a damned good attorney and you know it. I'll be faxing my resignation to the office in the morning." She left him gaping, looking like a landed fish gasping for air. And it wasn't until she'd unlocked her car, started it and began driving through the snowy streets to her grandmother's house that she realized what she'd done.

"So be it," she said to her reflection in the rearview mirror. It was time to start over. With or without Slade McCafferty.

"So what're you going to do about Jamie?" Randi asked as she padded into the living room. The house was dark, everyone having gone to bed, except Slade. He sat near the dying fire, glowering at the lopsided Christmas tree and remembering making love to Jamie in the hayloft. A drink sat on the table beside him but he didn't really want it. Randi, in a worn robe and fluffy slippers, settled into the rocker, cradled her son and smiled down at his little face. She cooed at him as she offered him a bottle. The baby played with the nipple and stared straight into his mother's face as if mesmerized.

"What do you mean, what am I going to do about her?"

Randi yawned. Her short hair stuck up at weird angles but her face, devoid of makeup looked healthy and fresh, no bruises or scars visible from the accident that had maimed her. "Let's not go over this again, okay? We both know that you've got it bad for the lady lawyer, and if you don't do something about it soon, you're going to lose her to the likes of Chuck Jansen."

"How can I lose what I haven't got?"

"Oh, give me a break. This is how I make my living, remember? I'm a professional."

"A professional who self-admittedly doesn't have all of her faculties."

She grinned, placing a foot on the hearth and gently rocking as the baby cooed and gurgled and continued to stare up at her as he suckled. "I know what I see. You love her. She loves you. End of story. It's simple." Before he could argue she pointed a long finger in his direction. "But she's not going to make the mistake of waiting around for you again. She did that once, and a woman like Jamie's got too much on the ball to make the same mistake twice."

He frowned, thought about their brief love affair and the baby he hadn't known existed. That was twice now that he'd lost an unborn child, and it hurt. It hurt like hell. Guilt, for living when his progeny had not, twisted his guts. He watched Randi play with her newborn and felt a pang. Would he ever have a son of his own? A daughter?

Not if you don't settle down, Slade. It's time.

235

Randi's right.

And his father — what was it John Randall had said to him? *Don't waste your life, son. It's shorter than you think. Now, it's time for you to move on. Settle down. Start a family.* He'd given that advice on the front porch, in the very rocker Randi was now seated in, on the day he'd tried to give Slade his watch. Slade had been angry. Mad at the world. Sick of his old man trying to manipulate him. In utter disdain, he'd dropped the damned timepiece into the old man's lap. He'd refused to take it; hadn't accepted it until John Randall had died. And then it was too late. He reached into his pocket for the watch and realized it was gone . . . but where? Then he remembered. In the hayloft, when he'd kicked off his jeans . . . it must've dropped into the loose straw when he'd been making love to Jamie . . . Hell.

As Randi swayed in the old rocking chair, Slade picked up his drink and tossed back the watered-down whiskey. It was smooth against his throat, but didn't quiet the rage in his soul.

"I don't know what she sees in Jansen," Randi said out loud. "He's too old for her and so . . . nothing. But maybe she's not looking for a spark, maybe she's looking for

236

security, maybe she's tired of being alone."

"Are you talking about Jamie or you?" Slade asked, wiping the back of his hand over his lips and setting the glass on the table. "I know you're used to being the one handing out advice, but I think it's a waste of time with me. I know what I want."

"I beg to differ, little brother." She lifted the baby to her shoulder and rubbed his back.

"I'm *not* your little brother," he reminded her.

"You're my youngest brother . . . you just happen to be older than me and bigger than me but surely not wiser."

"Tell me about it," he mocked. "I don't see that you've got everything all planned out."

"What do you mean?"

"Let's start with your son."

"Let's not."

"But, you have to admit, great as he is, it wasn't exactly perfect family planning on your part."

"You don't know what you're talking about."

Joshua gave up a loud burp. His little head bobbed, reddish hair glinting in the remaining firelight.

"There ya go," Randi said to her son,

before settling him into her arms again. "You know, Slade, we weren't talking about me, so don't turn this around. Let's talk about you. And our brothers. Look at Thorne. I always thought he was the ultimate bachelor. But he's married now. Happy. He and Nicole and the girls are a complete family, even though technically the twins have another biological father."

At the thought of Paul Stevenson, Slade snorted and considered another drink. What a jerk. Paul had remarried, still lived in San Francisco, and aside from sending an occasional check that Nicole deposited for the twins' college account, he never acknowledged his daughters. He didn't call, he didn't visit, he didn't ever have them come to spend time with him. Nicole had once called him a sperm donor and Slade agreed with her.

"Yeah, so Thorne's married, so what?"

"And Matt will be soon. He and Kelly are so happy —"

"So happy they're sickening."

Randi chuckled. "They're in love."

"I guess."

"I *know*. So, that leaves you."

"And you," he reminded her, and saw her bristle.

"I've got the baby. I don't need a man,

and don't argue with me. I see it in your eyes. You're one of those guys who thinks every woman needs a man. Or wants one. Or can't get by without one. But I don't. I can take care of myself."

"Well, you're doin' a helluva job of it. So far someone's tried to kill you twice." He pushed out of his chair and crossed the room to the rocker. Smiling, he reached down and patted the baby's downy little head. "The next time the creep, whoever he is, tries to nail you, you might not be so lucky. And, whether you want to admit it or not, you're not as independent as you like to claim. You've always depended on men.

"First there was Dad and now, when you're in trouble, you've got the three of us — half brothers — who think we need to do what we can to keep you safe." She looked up, her eyes glistening, then turned to the fire. "Contrary to what you think, *little* sister, you're not so tough, and maybe not every woman needs a man or vice versa, but sometimes it's nice to have one around."

"That's just what I was getting at." Her voice was a little gruffer than usual. "You could have that same love that our brothers have found. With Jamie. If you're not too stupid and bullheaded to throw it away again."

contempt

"Thanks for the advice," he muttered, unable to hide the derision in his voice as she sniffed back the unwanted tears. "I'll think about it."

His bad leg ached a little as he walked to the front door and snagged his jacket from a hook. Randi's advice chased after him as he stepped outside and a gust of raw Montana wind slapped him. Ice dripped from the eaves and snow continued to fall and swirl, the wind blowing it around. Drifts piled against the barns and fence.

Harold, the crippled old dog, trooped after Slade as he headed for the stables. He found his last cigarette in the crumpled pack; he swore it would be his last. No reason to let the filter tip go to waste.

Pausing near the machine shed, he turned his back to the wind, cupped his hands around the tip of the cigarette, and clicked his lighter about five times before a flame sparked. He inhaled and felt the warm smoke curl deep inside his lungs as he and the dog slogged through the unbroken snow to the stables. He'd finish his last smoke, then go inside and find his father's watch.

As he smoked and looked at the vast acres of the ranch, the fields and paddocks, ranch house and sheds, he understood why his father had loved it here. Maybe John Randall had been right about other things, as well. Maybe it was time to settle down. He thought of Jamie. Damned if she wasn't the right woman. If he hadn't blown it with her.

He took a final drag, tossed his cigarette into the snow and reached for the door.

First thing tomorrow, he'd find her and tell her how he felt. He yanked on the door handle.

Lightning flashed before his eyes.

Bam!

Slade flew backward. Landed hard on the snow.

A ball of flames roared to life. Hot. Bright. Blinding.

Horses squealed in terror.

Flames burst upward, crackling hungrily through the old timbers and dry hay. Smoke billowed into the cold night air.

Slade scrambled to his feet. Panicked horses kicked and shrieked. The entire building was ablaze.

He didn't have time to think.

He catapulted through the doorway.

And straight into hell.

CHAPTER TWELVE

Bam!

The sound was like a shock wave.

Randi bolted from the bed, picked up Joshua Ray and hauled him to the hallway.

"For God's sake, call 9-1-1! Use the damned cell phone, we've got to get out of here!" Thorne burst from the master bedroom. He packed a groggy twin in each arm. Frantic, he yelled over his shoulder, "Nicole! Come on!"

Randi struggled into shoes, her heart drumming a thousand times a minute. "What was that? Did you hear it? An explosion."

"I don't know what it was, but it's not good. Everyone outside!" Thorne screamed. "Nicole! Come on!"

His wife burst out of the bedroom. Her blond hair fell around her face as she struggled with the tie of her bathrobe with one hand. A cell phone was pinned to her ear with the other.

They trampled down the stairs.

"Where's Slade?" Thorne said as they reached the first floor.

"He was outside a few minutes ago. I just came upstairs," Randi said. Where the devil was he? The interior of the house began to turn a bright, vibrant orange. "What's going on?"

"Oh, God." Ushering everyone to the foyer, Thorne paused long enough to stare through the window. "It's the stables!" He shouldered open the door and they all streamed onto the porch. The old building was ablaze, orange and gold reflecting on the snow. Smoke poured from the roof where flames ate the old shingles and shot skyward.

"No!" Randi cried.

"Oh, my God . . ." Nicole's eyes were round.

"Get away from the house!" Thorne ordered. "Everyone!" He reached back through the doorway and yanked every coat from the rack, then, still carrying the girls, kicked boots and shoes onto the porch. "Hurry!"

The twins were crying now, clinging to his neck as Randi found a coat and dashed away from the house. Where was Slade?

Where the devil was Slade? Not in the stables. No . . . it couldn't be . . . And yet she'd seen him leave the house . . . Oh, God, oh, God, oh, God . . .

"— That's right at the Flying M ranch, twenty miles north of Grand Hope," Nicole was screaming into her cell phone. "We'll need firemen and rescue workers and . . . and a veterinarian and God knows what else! This is an emergency! I repeat, an emergency at the McCaffertys' Flying M ranch!"

The twins, ashen-faced and wide eyes, wailed. They buried their little faces into Thorne's shoulders and clung to his neck as if they would never let go.

"Was Slade in the stables?" Thorne demanded, his harsh gaze centering on Randi as they hurried toward the parking lot, away from the buildings.

"I don't know . . ." Randi stared at the inferno as the first horse burst out of the flaming building. White-eyed and sweating, the gray galloped crazily through the snow. A bay followed after, whistling, hooves flinging up white powder as she tried to escape the blaze. "I don't know where he went. We were talking in the living room, then, then . . . he went outside for a smoke." She stared in horror at the burning building.

"Well, someone's letting the stock out. Idiot!" Grim-faced, Thorne shoved both twins at Nicole as she flew out the door. The girls screamed their protests.

"No! Daddy! No."

"Here. Take the girls and don't go inside any of the buildings. None of them. The stables might just be the first. And — oh, damn!" He glanced at the cars and trucks. "Keep away from the vehicles in case there's some sort of chain reaction." His jaw tightened as he herded them to relative safety.

"I've got 'em," Nicole said, peeling each girl from their father's body.

"Chain reaction?" Randi asked.

His face was stretched taut. "You don't think this is an accident, do you?" He yelled over the screams of the horses and roar of the fire. Timbers creaked eerily and thick smoke bulged outward. Thorne started for the stables.

"Wait a minute. You can't go inside there," Randi cried. "It's too late."

"Thorne!" Nicole was running after him. Packing her girls, frantic, she stumbled forward. "Thorne! No! No!"

"Get back. Take care of the kids and call Matt!"

"No! Oh, God no! Wait for the firemen!" she pleaded, distraught as she clung to her children. "You can't —"

"It'll take too long." Thorne took a second to turn to stare at her horrified face. As if to memorize her features. "I'll be all right. You take care of the girls. Now!" Nicole took a step toward him, and Randi wanted to help. To hand the baby off to Nicole and brave the fire herself. Oh, God, was this her fault? Could this be because of her? Was it a freak accident . . . or a planned execution of some of the stock . . . and maybe a McCafferty or two?

Thorne spun again and a few seconds later nearly collided with a wild-eyed horse galloping out of the open doorway. Other animals burst from a door on the west end of the building, a mare and two foals, their tails singed, their screams blood-chilling.

The baby was crying, the girls screaming, and Randi tried to herd them all together. "It'll be all right," she said, though she didn't believe it.

"Daddy. Daddy! No-oo." Molly was sobbing; Mindy ashen-faced as she stared after her father.

Thorne disappeared into the doorway. Into the smoke and flames. Randi was shaking, but she said, "He's going to be fine."

Nicole's face was as pale as death, her eyes round with fear, but she visibly pulled herself together and held her daughters tight. "Daddy's gonna be just fine. He has to help Uncle Slade and the horses . . . see there . . . some of them are getting out now." She kissed each crown as Molly and Mindy cried all the more loudly. Nicole managed to hold on to her shivering children while punching the numbers of her cell phone frantically. "Matt? It's Nicole." Her voice was surprisingly steady. Probably from years of working in emergency rooms. Eyes fixed on the blaze, she said, "You'd better get over here. And bring help. There's been an explosion in the stables. It's on fire and it's bad. Some of the stock might be injured. I've called 9-1-1, rescue crews are on their way, but the building's in flames and . . . and both of your brothers are inside."

Slade coughed, stumbled through the smoke. He'd opened the main door and was going down the aisles, unlocking stalls, forcing panicked horses from their boxes. "Go! Out! Hiya!" he yelled, his eyes burning, the cloth he used to cover his nose and mouth no insulation against the blast of heat that singed his skin.

"Slade!" Thorne's voice screamed from somewhere through the smoke. "Slade!"

"You, out!" He held open a door but the

frightened mare reared, her hooves flashing, her coat soaked in lather. "Now!" Slade bellowed, and pushed at her. She kicked wildly, her muscles quivering. He slapped her rear and a leg shot out, narrowly missing him as she bolted. He fell against the rail.

Two more stalls. He flung himself down the aisle, aware of the creak of timbers, the crackle of flames, the roar of the fire itself. Moving blind, he made it to the next stall where Mrs. Brown, a spunky mare was shivering, the whites of her eyes visible. "It's okay, girl . . ." he said, his lungs on fire.

Timbers creaked ominously and the smoke . . . God, the smoke. He hacked and forced himself out of the stall.

"Slade! Damn it, where are you?" Thorne's voice was farther away. Slade tried to respond but his throat, filled with smoke and soot, wouldn't work. He kicked open the door, flailed at the horse and she shot through the stall door like a bullet.

One more. He stumbled forward. Saw the terrified animal. Diablo Rojo. Pacing. Rearing. Neighing in terror as flames crawled through the straw at his hooves. "Come on, boy," Slade tried to say, but the words stuck. Coughing, he threw open the door to the box and Red Devil lunged through the opening, a huge shoulder knocking Slade

248

off his feet. Crack. His head hit the floor.

"Slade! Oh, damn — *Slaaaaade!*"

He tried to pull himself to his feet. A spray of sparks showered from above. Rafters groaned and he thought of all the tons of hay overhead. He glanced up. A huge blackened beam began to crumble. Ah, hell!

Slade dived toward the window.

With a tremendous wrenching moan, the beam snapped.

All hell rained down.

"A fire. What do you mean, there's a fire?" Kelly demanded as Matt rolled out of the bed in her condo.

"In the stables at the ranch. Thorne and Slade might be trapped inside."

"No." Kelly couldn't believe it. She shook off sleep. "But . . . why? How?"

He was already throwing on clothes. "Nicole didn't say. Probably doesn't know, but I gotta get over there."

"I'm coming with you." She grabbed her sweatpants and a sweatshirt, then reached into a drawer for her .38.

"You don't need that."

"I hope not."

Matt didn't bother with a belt. "It might be safer for you to stay here."

"No way." She pulled on work boots, then

followed him out the door of the bedroom and down the stairs to the garage. They both grabbed jackets and climbed into his truck.

Kelly hit the electronic opener. Matt twisted on the ignition. As the garage door opened, the wail of sirens split the cold winter air.

"Fire trucks," Matt said.

"And an ambulance." Before she could buckle her seat belt he'd thrown the pickup into reverse. Cranking hard on the wheel, he backed into the parking space, then gunned it. Spraying snow and gravel, the pickup shot forward. Kelly grabbed her cell phone. "I'm calling Striker," she said. "And Espinoza."

On the third ring, a clear voice answered. "Striker."

"There's a fire at the McCafferty ranch. No one knows the cause, at least not that I'm aware of. Slade and Thorne could be trapped in the building. Emergency services have been called."

"I'm already on my way," Striker said. "I was on my way over there when I heard the call on the police band."

Kelly hung up as the wipers slapped snow from the windshield and Matt glowered at the road. He drove as if his life depended on it. As if his brothers' lives depended on it. "I should have stayed at the ranch."

"Oh, right. Then maybe you could be trapped in there, too."

"Maybe I could have prevented it."

Kelly checked to see that her pistol was loaded. "I don't know, Matt. I'm starting to think no one can prevent what's happening with your family."

"And you want to marry into it." He slid her a questioning glance.

"It takes more than this to scare me off." She flipped on the radio to a local news program. "Striker will be there in a few minutes."

"Not soon enough." Matt drove like a madman but Kelly didn't comment, just punched out the number for Detective Espinoza's home. Her heart felt like lead, her throat tight. Despite all her years of training on the force, she couldn't maintain a professional veneer of calm. Not when two men she'd grown to love, Matt's brothers, the men who would soon be a part of her family, were in danger.

Please let them be safe, she thought, reaching over and placing her hand on Matt's thigh. She needed to touch him, to be reassured, to believe that they would be safe.

"Yeah?"

"Bob. It's Kelly. I don't know if you've heard but there's been more trouble at the McCafferty ranch. The stables are on fire. According to Nicole McCafferty, her husband and brother-in-law Slade are trapped inside. She's already called 9-1-1. We're driving over there now and emergency crews are on the way."

"I'll be there . . . oh, I'm just getting a page. That must be the call." He clicked off.

"I don't suppose you know Jamie Parsons's number?" Kelly asked.

Matt frowned and shook his head.

"She'll want to know," Kelly added as the weather report reverberated through the speakers. "According to Nicole, Jamie's in love with Slade. Nicole's seen the way she looks at him."

Matt's fingers tightened on the wheel. He took a corner too fast and the truck skidded before its wide tires grabbed the road. "You could probably get hold of her through her grandmother's old number . . . well, unless they interrupted service. It would be under Nita Parsons, I think, or Anita."

Kelly dialed again, this time to directory assistance. After a few false starts, she located the number of Jamie's grandmother. Punching the numbers quickly, she watched through the windshield as the town of

Grand Hope sped by. Christmas lights reflected on the snow-blanketed streets, very little traffic disturbed the quietude, the peace and tranquility that accompanied the Christmas season.

Not far away, the sounds of sirens shrieked of impending doom.

The phone jangled. It sounded as if it came from a distance. Jamie stretched and frowned, pulled the covers over her head, then, finally, when the ringing didn't stop, realized where she was. The digital readout of her travel clock showed that it was after one in the morning. Above the soft hum of the furnace, she heard the sound of sirens wailing. Groggy, she rolled out of bed, banged her head and didn't bother with slippers as she made her way down the stairs to the kitchen.

Lazarus meowed and hurried after her as she finally picked up. "Hullo?" she mumbled, catching sight of her reflection in one of the panes above the sink. Her hair was tossed and wild, and she could detect smudges under her eyes from lack of sleep.

"Jamie? This is Kelly Dillinger. Matt's fiancée."

Jamie's heart stopped. *Slade!* Something had happened to him. She knew it.

"There's a fire at the ranch. The stables."

"What?" Her legs gave out and she slumped against the counter as her mind cleared.

"I don't want to alarm you, but there's a chance that Slade and Thorne might be inside." Jamie's knees gave way. She slid down the cabinets to sit on the floor. A million questions raced through her mind. This had to be a dream — a horrid nightmare . . . that was it. "Emergency crews are on their way."

"Wait a minute . . . there must be some mistake," Jamie said, almost pleading.

"I wish there were." There was a pause and Jamie started to shake. The sirens sounded farther away. Oh, God. It couldn't be.

"No," she whispered.

"I just thought you'd want to know," Kelly said.

"I can't believe it."

"I know . . . and . . . Slade's probably safe. I haven't tried calling the ranch again. We got the call about ten minutes ago, so things could've changed by now."

But Jamie heard the doubt in Kelly's voice. "I — I'll be there."

"That's probably not a good idea. It'll be chaos. I just thought you'd want to know.

So why don't you wait there? We'll call you. Really. Stay put. I'll keep you informed. Will you be okay?"

Jamie didn't answer. She hung up and took the stairs two at a time. She threw on the first clothes she found, grabbed her keys, then raced down the stairs again. She was out the door and in her car within seconds.

This couldn't be happening. Not to Slade. No, no, no! Her fingers shook as she jammed the key into the ignition and cranked the defroster to high. She didn't wait for the window to clear, just twisted on the wipers and with her head hanging out the driver's window, drove like crazy. Her car slid and skidded. She didn't care. She blinked against the snow, swore as she slid on the bridge, then floored it. Tires spun. The wind slapped her face and she blinked as the defroster and wipers cleared the windshield.

She nosed her little car north toward the Flying M, toward a glimmer of light, a bright orange glow that cut through the snowstorm. "God help us," she whispered, then drove as if Satan himself were following.

■ ■ ■ ■

"Slade! For God's sake, where the hell are you?"

Slade heard Thorne's voice, tried to shout but could only moan and cough. The timber that pinned him down singed his back and fire danced in front of his eyes. He tried to drag himself out from under the heavy weight, his hands clawing at the hot cement. He didn't so much as budge. It was too late. "Get out," he tried to scream to his brother. Heat as intense as a blast furnace poured over him. The fire raged, flames crawling everywhere.

He thought of Jamie. "I love you," he mouthed, envisioning her face. Would he ever see her again?

A window splintered. Shards of glass spattered. Somewhere too far away, over the roar of the blaze, sirens screamed. Help was on the way. Too little. Too late.

Get out, Slade. Don't give up! The voice in his head nagged him as the fire stormed. With all his effort he reached forward, straining, stretching, until he heard his tendons pop. Pain shrieked up his spine. He grabbed hold of the lowest rail of a stall. Inside the box the straw ignited. Gritting his teeth, he pulled. Hard. His muscles rebelled. Agony ripped through him. The heat was unbearable, the smoke thick. He began to pass out, his vision blurring from the outside in . . .

"Hang on!" Thorne yelled.

"Get the hell out of here," he croaked.

"Not without you."

The building shuddered and another flaming beam crash-landed two feet from Slade's head. Burning splinters flew crazily. Bales tumbled down. Dust exploded. Smoke billowed. From somewhere nearby, choking and gasping, Thorne appeared.

His face was covered in soot, his eyes searching the inferno until his gaze landed on his brother.

"Let's go."

Sirens shrieked. The rumble of huge engines — fire trucks — was barely audible over the blaze.

"Come on —" Thorne grabbed hold of Slade's shoulders, tried to pull, got nowhere. "Slade, come on . . ." Choking and gasping, Thorne let go, yanked an ax from the wall and while Slade barely hung on to consciousness, threw his weight into a swing. The beam shuddered. Pain screeched through Slade. The world swam in darkness.

Thorne swung again, coughing, nearly

doubling over, then threw his weight into it again, jarring Slade, hacking at the beam. "Hang in there!" Thorne yelled as the flames hissed. *Cra-a-ack.* The timber split. Thorne threw down the ax, grabbed Slade by the arms and dragged him toward the open double doors.

Another window burst. Glass sprayed. Air rushed. Flames licked around them. Slade tried to move his legs, but they were dead weights, wouldn't so much as flinch.

"Help out here," Thorne demanded as he pulled Slade outside. Cold air swept over him and in his blurry vision he saw the flash of red and blue lights strobe the night. Firemen in slick suits carried hoses, aimed huge nozzles at the stables and shouted orders. Horses galloped madly throughout the property, generally getting in the way. A group of people, his family, was gathered on the front lawn. Safe. Thank God.

"Is he the last one?" a fireman asked.

"I — I think so," Thorne said as Slade fought the urge to pass out. He willed his eyes open, but the pain in his back brought the blackness again. Coughing, feeling as if his lungs were charred, Slade looked toward the ranch house and saw Jamie.

Running through the snow toward him, tears streaming down her face, her hair wild and streaming behind her, she ignored the shouts of firemen and police to stay back.

"Slade," she cried, her voice dim in the cacophony. "Slade . . . oh, God!" Two ranch hands chased after her. But she was determined and as she reached him she fell to her knees, her tears raining upon him. He tried to smile, to form her name, but he couldn't move and the blackness, sweet and enticing, promising freedom from pain, finally closed over him.

"Help him!" Jamie cried as she witnessed Slade drifting away. One minute he was staring up at her, alive, breathing. The next, his eyes closed. "Oh, God, no . . ."

"Excuse us, ma'am." Big arms pulled her back as a team of rescue workers, EMTs, worked over Slade and Thorne, who, after the supreme effort of pulling his brother to safety had fallen in a heap in the snow. Like Slade's, Thorne's jacket and hair were singed, his face lacerated and blackened, but he was awake, barking orders while Slade . . . Oh, Lord . . . Slade was immobile, unresponsive and as a team of rescue workers and Nicole began to tend to him, they pushed her further to the background.

Jamie heard pieces of the conversation, his blood pressure, heart rate . . . other statistics as they hooked him to tubes and carried him on a stretcher to the waiting ambulance. Nicole was helping Thorne to his feet and he was limping, but insisting that he didn't need a stretcher as they made their way across the snowy yard. The sheriff's department had arrived and deputies, the firemen and ambulance workers were trying to contain the blaze, the horses, and keep everyone safe.

"Are you all right?"

Jamie turned and stared at Kurt Striker, not immediately recognizing the private detective in his hooded ski jacket.

"Yes . . . I guess . . . But, Slade . . ." She swallowed hard as she watched the EMTs load him into the ambulance.

"They're taking him to St. James Hospital."

"Then I have to go." She started for her car, but he held on to her arm.

"Why don't you ride with Nicole? She's driving Thorne." Striker motioned to one of the trucks owned by the Flying M. Nicole was helping Thorne into the cab.

Pull yourself together, Jamie. Obviously this man thinks you're out of it. A horse raced by, galloping to join some of the herd. Randi was holding her baby and talking to Kelly Dillinger who was shepherding the twins as they cried and pointed to the pickup.

"I'm not sure you should drive," Striker was saying.

Jamie glanced back to the truck. Nicole was already at the wheel. With a roar, the engine sparked to life and wipers tackled the snow on the windshield. "I can drive myself." She pulled open her car door, determined to follow the ambulance to the hospital. To be near Slade.

"Are you sure you're okay?" Matt was asking this time, his dark eyes penetrating from beneath the brim of his Stetson. "There's plenty of room in Thorne's truck. I'd drive you myself, but I've got to stay here awhile until the bomb squad has searched the place." He looked at Striker. "The police think the fire might have been arson and want to know that the house isn't booby-trapped."

"What? Bomb squad? Booby-trapped? It wasn't an accident?" Jamie asked, stunned.

"Probably not," Kurt said.

"Someone intentionally did this?" She swept an arm to include the stables, now soaked with water, the flames sizzling and sending up deep clouds of steam with the smoke. "How do you know so soon? I mean . . ." She stared at what was left of the charred, gutted building and the fire that was slowly beginning to die.

"Gut instinct," Striker said, pushing gloved hands deep into his pockets as he eyed the house. His gaze dropped to Randi and the girls, and his jaw visibly tightened. "I think this is another attempt to warn the McCaffertys, especially Randi."

"By killing horses?" That didn't make sense.

"*Her* horses. She owns half the ranch."

The ambulance, lights flashing angrily, took off.

"Matt owns half the ranch, as well," Jamie said. "Or will soon." She wasn't letting out any information that Striker didn't already have.

"I know, but no one's made an attempt on my life before and Randi's seems to be a target for some nutcase." Matt glowered into the night.

"So you think that whoever started this fire was warning Randi to back off of something?"

"Could be," Striker said.

"I think he's right." Matt looked over at his nieces and fiancée. "I'd better help out with the girls." He looked over at Randi, who was clutching J.R. With Kelly's help, Randi was to ride herd over the twins who continued to sob and cry even after their parents had driven off. Snow swirled around

262

them. Kelly leaned down and picked up one little girl while Matt ran through the trampled yard and snagged the other off her feet. Jamie felt cold to the bottom of her soul. Who would want to harm this family? "What could Randi be doing that would make someone want to kill her or her child or the livestock?"

"That's what I have to find out," Striker admitted as he gazed at the horses, calmer now, ears flicking as they huddled together on the far side of the house. "Before anyone else gets hurt."

Jamie stared down the lane. The ambulance lights flashed through the trees and her heart twisted. Slade was inside . . . but surely he would pull through. She slid behind the wheel of her compact and twisted the key in the ignition. She'd always thought of Slade McCafferty as indestructible.

Now she prayed that she was right.

CHAPTER THIRTEEN

Dawn was still a few hours off. Through the windows of St. James Hospital, Jamie stared into the darkness, to the parking lot of the hospital. The snow had stopped falling.

And not a word about Slade.

Her stomach in knots, Jamie leaned against the windowsill and swirled powdered cream into her tepid coffee. She knew he was alive. Certainly someone would have told her if he wasn't okay. But how long could it take?

Glancing at the double doors of the hospital emergency room for the zillionth time, she willed someone, anyone — doctor, nurse aide — to appear and give her a sliver of information. All she knew was that aside from the smoke inhalation and burns, his back was involved.

Broken?

God, no. She couldn't think that way. She looked at the clock for the tenth time in as many minutes. What was taking so long? She hadn't heard a word on Thorne, either. Where was Nicole? Why didn't she appear with some kind of information?

Because she's with her husband. Standing by the man she loves. Where you should be, if you could.

Jamie paced from one end of the small waiting room to the other, then rested a hip against the wide ledge of a window again. She'd arrived five minutes later than the ambulance, hadn't gotten so much as a peek at Slade, and the hospital staff was being tight-lipped. She wasn't family.

She sipped the horrible sludge in her cup without really tasting it. She'd been up for hours, was bone-weary, but knew that if she went home, she wouldn't be able to sleep. Not with Slade here. Not without knowing about his condition.

Surely he would pull through. He was a McCafferty; they were all tough as old leather and had more lives than the proverbial cat. Right? Then why did she have a cold feeling in the middle of her stomach, a knot of fear that wouldn't go away?

She remembered him swinging the ax and splitting kindling for her that first night they were alone together. Then there were images of him cutting down the Christmas tree and driving the sleigh, mental pictures of him holding Randi's baby or playing with his nieces. And, of course, the more recent memory of being with him, of gazing into his eyes as he'd peeled off her clothes and made love to her in the very building where he'd been nearly crushed to death and burned alive.

Her throat ached. She wanted to break down, but wouldn't. Couldn't. He might need her.

When pigs fly, Jamie. When has he ever needed you?

Now, she thought determinedly. He needs me now!

He would be all right.

He had to be.

She dropped into one of the chairs.

"Jamie!" Chuck's voice rang down the empty corridor and she looked up to see him breezing toward the waiting room. Four-seventeen in the morning and he was clean shaven, not a hair out of place, dressed in pressed khakis, the sweater she'd given him last Christmas and a wool overcoat. As if he were going to the damned golf course. All he needed was one of those funny little caps. "I just heard what happened."

"How?" she asked. Why hadn't he been sleeping?

"Cell phone. Matt called from the ranch. Thought I'd want to know what was going on." His smile seemed genuine, his eyes kind. "Thorne McCafferty is a friend of mine, you know."

That's right. All of Chuck's friends were business associates in one way or another. She closed her eyes for a second, hated to be so cynical. "And Matt was concerned about you. He and . . . oh, what's her name?" Chuck asked.

"Kelly?"

"Yeah, the wife-to-be will be here as soon as they've got things handled at the ranch. I think the sister will be here, too. Something about waiting for a baby-sitter or the house-keeper, or someone to look after the kids."

"Good."

"Are you all right?" Was there genuine concern in Chuck's voice?

"Holding my own," Jamie said, though she knew she must look a wreck. Not that she cared. She shoved her hair from her eyes and glanced at the clock again.

"And Thorne?" Chuck's expression grew more serious.

"He'll be all right, I think, though I haven't heard . . . I expected Nicole to come out and explain what was going on."

"From what Matt said, Slade was injured

more seriously. Thorne went in to save him."

"That's what I've heard . . . Slade ran into the stables to save the stock, so he was in there the longest . . . I really don't know what happened, just that Thorne dragged him out of the fire and Slade lost consciousness."

Chuck took a seat on the arm of her chair. His hands were clasped between his knees. "You're in love with him, aren't you?"

Jamie nodded, shook her head, then sighed. "I think so . . . yes. I mean —"

"I get the picture. Oh, Jamie." There was pain in Chuck's voice as he gazed at her for a minute, touched her shoulder, then, as if aware of the tenderness of the gesture, stood suddenly. "I always knew it wasn't quite right between us. I wasn't what you wanted, but I was hoping . . ." He lifted a hand, then let it drop. "Well, I just hope you know what you're doing."

"I do, Chuck."

"Then good luck." He seemed as if he was about to say something more when the double doors swung open.

Jamie shot to her feet. Nicole, disheveled, her expression grim, swept through the opening. "Sorry I didn't get to you any earlier," she said as Jamie met her halfway across the waiting area.

"Slade?"

"He's going to live," she said, her amber eyes dark with pain. Then, as if quickly donning her professional persona, she squared her shoulders and added, "The surface stuff, cuts and bruises, will heal quickly. He's got some second-degree burns on his hands and face, but, that, too, isn't what's of the most concern."

"What?" Jamie asked.

"It's his back, Jamie. One vertebra is cracked and there could be some damage to his spinal cord." Jamie's knees threatened to give way.

Chuck grabbed her arm, but she made herself stand and forced the hated words over her tongue. "How much damage?" she asked, not daring to think about the possibility that Slade might be paralyzed.

"We don't know. Bruised for certain, maybe just pinched, probably not severed." She began talking in medical terms that Jamie, had she not been fighting the buzz of fear thrumming through her brain, or the denial that threatened to rise in her throat, might have understood. But all she could think about was seeing Slade again. Touching him. Telling him that she loved him.

"Is he conscious?"

"Not yet."

"And the prognosis?" Chuck asked as a cart, wheeled by a balding male aide, rattled past.

"It's too early to tell. But Dr. Nimmo is an excellent neurosurgeon and he's linked via computer to the best in the country. I can assure you that Slade is getting the best possible care."

"When can I see him?" Jamie asked.

"Not until the doctors have finished. That might be a while." Nicole placed a hand on Jamie's sleeve. "Why don't you go home for a while? Rest. There's nothing to be done here and I promise I'll call you myself if there's any change."

"I want to stay," Jamie insisted.

"Why? It serves no purpose. Won't help." Chuck gave her one of his now-let's-be-reasonable looks, the one where one of his silver eyebrows raised slightly as he looked at her from the tops of his eyes.

"I'll feel better about it if I'm close by."

Chuck sighed. "He doesn't even know you're here."

"That's right," Nicole said. "It would be best if you got some sleep."

"I'll doze here." Jamie was adamant. Her gaze touched the other woman's and she saw a spark of understanding in Nicole's eyes. She didn't have to say, *If things were* reversed and it was Thorne battling for his life, where would you be? "If there's any change, you'll let me know."

"Yes." Nicole nodded and offered an encouraging smile. "The second it occurs."

"Thanks."

"Now wait a minute . . ." Chuck tried to talk her into going back to Nana's place, but Jamie was determined to stay.

"You can't change my mind and that's that," she finally said, and rested her hips on the window ledge again. Chuck gave up, said something about going down to the cafeteria to try to scrounge up breakfast. Jamie wasn't hungry. She glanced at the clock again, saw the precious seconds sweeping by and realized she'd spent too many years running away from the truth that she loved Slade McCafferty. She always had. She probably always would.

"You have to face it, Randi, someone's sending you one helluva message." Kurt Striker's voice was harsh, his green eyes jade-cold as he watched her descend the stairs.

Damn the man, why was he hounding her now — when all hell had broken loose? She brushed past him on her way to the living room. The bomb squad had dispersed, declaring the house safe. The fire in the stables had been extinguished, leaving charred, soggy remains. The police vehicles and fire trucks had departed, but yellow crime scene tape now roped off the still smoldering building. Matt had called Larry Todd and the foreman had rushed over. The two men and Kelly had dealt with the frightened livestock, rounding up the crazed horses and finding shelter for them in the barn.

It was such a nightmare. Slade and Thorne were in the hospital, two of the horses had died, the ranch was a shambles, the children distraught.

While Kelly Dillinger should have been planning her wedding to Matt, she'd been chasing after terrorized livestock in the middle of the night and worrying herself sick over the men who were to become her brothers-in-law.

And the kids . . . It had taken hours but Randi had finally gotten the children into bed.

"Did you hear me? This is about you, you know." Striker wasn't giving up. But then, from what she'd heard of him, he never did. Dressed in Levis and a sheepskin-lined denim jacket, he was standing near the fireplace where he'd managed to stoke the

272

dying embers into flames. The familiar room looked cozy and secure, yet all she had to do was glance past the Christmas tree, through the window, to the destruction beyond.

"I'm not convinced it has anything to do with me. It could have been an accident."

"I talked with the fire chief. They're about ninety percent certain it was arson. They even think there was a trip wire to the door. When Slade opened it, he didn't have a chance."

"Oh, God."

Kurt crossed the room so that he was standing toe-to-toe with her. "You could be right. Even if the fire was arson, maybe it had nothing to do with you. Maybe the Flying M was a random target, maybe the arsonist has a grudge against someone else in your family, but, given what else has been happening in your life, I think the odds are against it." He rubbed the back of his neck, but his gaze never left hers. "I don't think you're willing to play God with your brothers' lives, with your nieces' lives, or with your son's life."

"Of course not!" Her nerves were strung tight, her emotions raw, her brain running in circles so fast that she couldn't sleep though she was exhausted. She didn't need

Striker with his accusations and suspicions. Not right now.

"All I'm asking is that you help us nail the bastard who's behind all this."

"Don't you think I would if I could?"

He didn't answer and she tipped her chin up so that she could impale him with her self-righteous glare. "I'll do everything possible. Of course I will." She was angry now, tired of the silent stares, the accusations. "What is it you want to know?"

"Everything, Randi. Everything you can remember about your life before your accident. I want to know what you were working on for the Seattle *Clarion.* I want to know if you were writing a book and what it was about. I want to know why you fired Larry Todd. I want to know why you were on that road in Glacier Park. And I want to know the name of the father of your child."

She swallowed hard and, as if he sensed resistance, he grabbed her arm with unforgiving fingers.

"No more lies, okay? No more half-truths. No more faked amnesia. We don't have time for any of that bull. Slade and Thorne are lucky to have gotten out of the fire alive. You and your son are lucky you survived the accident. It's probably a miracle of God you weren't killed in the hospital. But your luck might not hold. The next time someone might die."

Someone had taken a sledgehammer and was pounding it against his brain. And that same someone had decided that his lungs would feel better if they were on fire. Then Slade remembered. In terrifying Technicolor.

The fire. The horses. Thorne's voice and the beam splitting to pin him against the floor. The expression on Jamie Parsons's face when she'd seen him being dragged from the burning building.

He opened a bleary eye and saw metal rails. Beyond that were curtains — no, privacy drapes that sufficed as walls, and monitors surrounding him. He was in St. James Hospital, ICU, if he had to guess. Where Randi had recently been.

"Mr. McCafferty?"

He focused on a round-faced nurse who was staring down at him. She smiled benignly as she touched his arm. "How're you feeling?"

"Like hell," he rasped, but his throat was raw and the words barely passed his lips. His face felt cracked, dry, his arms like dead weights. There was a pain in the center of his back and his legs . . . what the hell? He tried to sit up.

"Whoa, there, we'll adjust the medication for your pain," she advised. "I've already called the doctor. He should be in to see you very shortly."

But there was something in her eyes, something he didn't trust. He tried to move his leg, but nothing happened. He attempted again. "My legs . . ." He looked down, saw them stretched out beneath the sheets.

"You've had some trauma to your back. As I said, the doctor will be in to talk to you about it."

"Trauma?" He gritted his teeth, tried to budge his damned legs, felt sweat bead on his skin. What was the issue she was dancing around? Trauma to his back. "You mean, to my spinal cord?"

"The doctor will be in —"

"Like hell. Are you telling me I'm paralyzed?" he demanded, the rest of his life flashing ahead of him. He saw wheelchairs, aides to help him do everything from bathe to urinate, to help him dress. No. He wouldn't believe it.

The nurse's lips pursed.

"Get me the doctor. Now!" he bellowed, though the words came out in a harsh, damning whisper. "And get my sister-in-law, Dr. Nicole Stevenson, er, McCafferty."

Another nurse appeared at the foot of his bed as he pushed himself upright. "Doctor ordered a sedative."

"I don't want a damned sedative. Hell's bells, you're telling me that I'm paralyzed, and now you want to knock me out?" He forced himself to a full sitting position, bracing himself with his hands, staring down at the useless limbs hidden by the crisp bed sheets and thin coverlet.

"Mr. McCafferty, please — just calm down and —"

Gritting his teeth he glared at his legs and willed them to move. Nothing. As the nurses adjusted his IV, he yanked off the coverings and saw beneath the short gown nothing out of the ordinary — two somewhat hairy legs that just wouldn't move. He panicked, then calmed. This was a nightmare, that was it. He was dreaming. He'd wake in his own bed and find out that everything was the same. The stables would be standing, all the horses, including Diablo Rojo waiting impatiently to be fed . . . so why the hell wouldn't his legs move?

"Where the hell is the doctor?" He glared at the nurse. "You call him now and . . . and . . ."

He felt suddenly drowsy. The words died

in his throat. His arms gave out and he flopped against the pillows as a door flew open and Nicole appeared.

"Slade? How are you?"

"You tell me," he said, though he had trouble wrapping his tongue around the words. God, he was tired. He wanted to close his eyes, to sink back into black oblivion and know that when he awoke everything would be the same. "Am . . . am I paralyzed?"

Gold eyes held his for a second. "We don't know the extent of damage to your spinal cord just yet," she said, and he felt as if a thousand-pound weight had been dropped on his chest. "It's too early to tell. Dr. Nimmo is doing everything he can. He's consulting with other specialists."

"But . . . there's chance . . ." He couldn't stay awake. Cool fingers surrounded his wrist.

"Let's not borrow trouble," Nicole said as his eyelids lowered and he envisioned for a second what his life would be like as a cripple . . . no that wasn't politically correct . . . a handicapped person . . . physically challenged . . . For a second Jamie's face came to mind. Beautiful. Smart. Successful. An attorney, for God's sake. A woman who had once been pregnant with his child . . .

but if he was paralyzed, he wouldn't be able to father children, to make love . . . he remembered the feel of her beneath him, the way her eyes had shone as she'd looked up at him . . . and as the blackness overcame him he realized he'd never make love to her again.

"I want to see him." No longer tired, adrenaline shooting through her veins as she heard Slade had been conscious, she was on her feet and squaring off with Nicole. Chuck had taken Thorne back to the ranch but Nicole had stayed to consult with the neurologist and to keep Jamie informed about Slade's condition. "If he's awake and can have a visitor, I want to see him."

Nicole frowned slightly. "Slade's sleeping now, he was only conscious for a few minutes. He's in a lot of pain so the doctor had standing orders for a sedative."

"I don't care," Jamie said, refusing to back down an inch. She'd spent the past five hours waiting for a glimpse of him, to know that he'd recover, praying that he'd survive, and she wasn't about to leave now. "Look, Nicole, please try to understand. I need to see him. I know I'm not family, but I thought you could see that I got inside."

"I could," Nicole hedged. She was wearing a lab coat and a worried expression that caused tiny lines to appear between her eyebrows.

"Then let's go."

"Are you sure you're ready for this?"

"Absolutely."

"You can't stay more than a couple of minutes."

Jamie took in a deep breath. "I understand."

"Okay, I'll do it, but only on one condition. You see Slade for a couple of minutes, then I want you to go home and get some rest." Nicole offered a tentative smile. "Doctor's orders."

"Fine. Anything. Just get me into his room."

Nicole hitched her chin toward the elevator. "ICU's on three. His 'room' is part of the ward, divided by curtains. I'll take you up there, make sure no one hassles you."

"Thanks." They rode up in the elevator in silence and Jamie, desperate to see for herself that Slade was alive, that he would make it, braced herself.

Still, she wasn't prepared for the sight of him.

Slade, bandaged, was lying immobile in a bed while tubes and wires ran into and out of his body. A shock of singed black hair fell over his forehead and cuts and abrasions sliced through his skin, some crossing the scar running down the side of his face. Burn marks — probably from cinders and sparks — were visible. "Oh, God," she whispered, her hand flying to her lips before she grabbed hold of herself.

"Are you okay? Sure you can handle this?" Nicole asked.

Jamie nodded mutely, steeled herself.

"Then I'll give you a minute alone with him." Nicole wandered a few feet to the nurse's station, the hub from which all the sectioned, curtained "rooms" spoked.

Biting her lower lip, Jamie walked to the edge of the bed, to a spot near his head, her fingers curling over the cold steel rails. "Slade," she said, her voice catching as she looked down at the strong angles of his face. Eyelashes curved against his cheekbones, his breathing was slow, but sure. "It's Jamie. I came to see how you were doing." Tears filled her eyes and her throat caught. She'd thought him indestructible with his sexy smile, devil-may-care attitude, and damned independent streak. Now, here he lay. Broken. Unconscious. Maybe never able to walk again. She picked up his hand, laced her fingers through his, and fought the urge to cry.

"You're gonna be okay," she said roughly, inwardly cringing as she heard the platitude in her voice, knowing she might be lying.

She couldn't see Slade confined to a wheelchair; this man who'd spent his life helicopter skiing, mountain climbing, bronc busting or white-water rafting. He'd been a hunting guide, raced cars, even been a stuntman. How could he adapt?

Don't give up on him. He'll be able to handle it. He's a McCafferty. Lord knows they're resilient. In no time he'd find a way to whip his wheelchair around the Flying M, to ride a horse, to shoot the rapids. He wouldn't let a disability beat him. This is Slade you're talking to. For God's sake, don't write him off.

Her voice was a little stronger. "You know, cowboy, there's something I've been meaning to tell you." The words formed in her heart but lodged in her throat. Giving his hand a squeeze, she forced them out. "I love you, Slade. I think . . . I know this sounds crazy, but I do think that a part of me has always loved you." She studied his face, so peaceful as he slept, so handsome and still, his jaw dark with beard shadow, bruises forming under his eyes. "I'll be here, when you wake up."

He didn't so much as twitch. No rapid eye movement behind his lids, no tentative squeeze of his fingers, no quick intake of breath. No flutter of his eyelids and, because of her words, no miraculous healing.

She saw Nicole looking in her direction. Knew her time was up. "I'll be back," she promised as she blinked away tears. "Don't go anywhere." Gently she dropped his hand onto the bedsheet. Wiping her eyes with the back of her hand, she met Nicole's gaze, then, fearing she'd break down all together, strode swiftly to the door.

"He'll get better," Nicole said as she caught up with her in the hallway.

"When?" Jamie snapped, then bit her tongue. Before Nicole could respond, Jamie held up a hand. "I'm sorry. I — you were right. It's hard to deal with. Thanks for letting me see him."

Nicole smiled, but her eyes were glassy with unshed tears. "Go home and get some sleep. Maybe when you wake up, Slade will be back to his normal cantankerous self and we'll have figured out who torched the stables. I'll call you if anything changes."

"Thanks again." They walked to the elevator and Jamie pushed the call button. She had to ask the question burning in her mind. "So, in your opinion as a doctor, what are the chances that Slade will walk again?"

"That I don't know," Nicole said, honesty

showing in her weary features, "but I'm certain he's getting the best care available. I would trust my life and my daughters' lives to Dr. Nimmo." She offered Jamie a tiny, tired smile. "Besides that, Slade's a McCafferty. If anyone was going to pull through this, it would be Slade." She tucked a stray strand of hair behind her ear. "He's suffered worse. He was almost killed once before, just last winter in the skiing accident. You know about that, don't you?"

Jamie nodded. "He told me."

"I wasn't in the family then, of course, but Thorne told me about it later. It wasn't so much his injuries, though they were bad enough, but when Rebecca and the baby didn't make it, he was lost. Despondent. He kind of dropped out of sight for a while. He blamed himself though no one could have talked Rebecca out of skiing that day."

Jamie froze. Slade had been a father? His child had died? Her heart crumbled. "They took the baby skiing?" she whispered, suddenly cold to the marrow of her bones.

"No . . . Rebecca was pregnant, somewhere between four and five months along, I think . . ." Nicole winced as if she'd realized she'd given away a confidence. "I thought he told you about this."

"I didn't know about the baby." Dear God, Slade had lost another unborn child? No wonder his reaction had been so violent when she'd told him about her own pregnancy. "I only knew that he'd lost someone dear to him, someone he loved." No wonder he'd been so upset in the hayloft. Dear God, had that been just yesterday? It seemed a lifetime ago.

The elevator arrived with a soft chime. The doors slid open. Her mind spinning, Jamie stepped inside.

"I'll keep you posted," Nicole assured her. "I promise." She lifted a hand as the doors whispered shut and Jamie sagged against the handrail. *Another baby. He'd lost another baby.* What were the odds of that? Her heart ached for him and for the child he'd never met — the two children.

The elevator stopped on the first floor and she walked on wooden legs toward the front door. As she stepped into the parking lot, she looked upward to the third floor and the windows she thought might be a part of ICU. Shivering and wrapping her coat more tightly around her, she noticed a stray piece of straw . . . a remnant from their lovemaking. A few flakes of snow began to fall in the early morning light. Jamie unlocked her car and slid inside. As she switched on the ignition, she prayed that Slade McCafferty would walk again.

CHAPTER FOURTEEN

You know, cowboy, there's something I've been meaning to tell you . . . I love you, Slade. I think . . . I know this sounds crazy, but I do think that a part of me has always loved you. I'll be here, when you wake up.

Jamie? Had Jamie been here? In his room? Or . . . where? Where the devil was he? He moaned, felt a shooting pain in his back and opened an eye.

It all came crashing back. He was in the hospital. There had been a fire. The horses . . . yeah, that was it, and he'd woken up earlier . . . Oh, God.

No! He tried to roll over, tried to lift a leg and . . . nothing. His mind was instantly clear. Pain screamed from the base of his skull, down his back and then just stopped. "Get me a doctor," he roared, his voice booming through the drapes to the station where a slim woman was bending over a chart. She looked up, her short brown hair neat, a patient smile tacked to her face. "Mr. McCafferty," she said, rounding the desk that looked as if it belonged at the helm of something out of *Star Wars*. "I wondered when you'd wake up."

"I want a doctor."

"Dr. Nimmo will be in this morning. How're you feeling?"

"How do you think I'm feeling?" he snarled, frustrated. "My damned legs won't move."

"I thought the nurse from the night shift explained that you've been in some trauma."

"I know that. What I don't know is how much damage there is. Am I going to be a cripple?"

She looked at him with kind eyes. "Let's not think that way, okay? Positive thoughts."

"I don't feel very positive," he rasped, his throat burning with the effort.

"Try." With the efficiency of years on the job, Slade watched her as she checked his temperature, blood pressure and pulse . . . which seemed overkill as there were half a dozen machines monitoring every bodily function known to man.

"Get my sister-in-law. Nic— Dr. Nicole McCafferty." God, his throat ached.

"I already paged her when I noticed you were rousing."

"Has anyone been in here? To see me?" he asked, wanting to know if Jamie had actually been at his bedside or if he'd dreamed it. The thought of her standing over him, knowing that his spine was injured . . .

"Dr. McCafferty's been in three times and your brother, Thorne, and someone Dr. Mc-Cafferty introduced as a family friend. A woman."

So it was true. Hell. She had been standing over him, knowing that he might never use his legs again, seeing him as half the man he was. His jaw tightened. He remembered making love to her in the hayloft. No wonder she'd said what she did. That she loved him. Bull. She felt obligated, as if in being with him in the stables she'd sealed her fate and now had to tie herself to a cripple. Which was ridiculous. And downright pathetic. He didn't want her feeling any sort of debt to him and he certainly didn't want her pity. God, he couldn't stand that.

The doors to ICU opened and he saw Nicole, looking as if she hadn't slept in days, sweep into the room. "Look who woke up," she chirped, offering him a smile that warmed her eyes. "Sleeping Beauty."

"Yeah, right," he grunted around the pain in his throat. "How's Thorne?"

"Fine. No serious damage. Minor burns and cuts. He'll live . . . Now, about you . . ."

"Yeah, about me. I can't move my damned legs. I've tried. Everyone is trying to placate me and pretend that everything's just hunky-dory and all the while they're mentioning things like cracked vertebrae, spinal trauma or spinal distress or even spinal bruising . . . I've heard them talking when I surfaced a time or two." He saw the darkness in his sister-in-law's gaze and her smile slid quietly from her face. "Tell it to me straight, Nicole. Am I going to be a cripple for the rest of my life?"

"I don't know." She sighed and met his gaze. "I won't lie to you. There's always that possibility, but the extent of the damage to your spine hasn't been established. Dr. Nimmo will be in soon. He's been consulting with his colleagues, and he's kept me apprised of your condition. He thinks you'll recover, at least partially, but I think it would be best if he talked to you himself."

"Then get him the hell in here."

"I will . . . the nurse has already called him and told him you were awake, but there's someone else who wants to see you. I promised Jamie I'd call her the minute you woke up. She's on her way. I'm meeting her in my office in fifteen minutes."

Slade's heart soared for a second, then he remembered her vows of love, whispered to a man near death, a man who might never be able to love her physically, a man to whom she felt indebted. Before the accident she'd insisted that what they'd shared all those years ago was nothing more than a quick fling, a "blip," sexual experimentation by two wild kids, nothing more. But then she made love to him and told him about the baby; he'd felt something change. Had it been love? Nah. No way. During their last conversation, they'd been standing in the snow by her car, spewing words of anger.

You're not seriously considering marrying that pompous ass, are you? Slade had asked and her response still rang through his head. *I was thinking about it, yes.*

The guy was a condescending jerk.

So now Slade was supposed to believe that she loved him? Damn it all to hell, he wasn't that much of a fool. He wouldn't let her guilt or pity or whatever the hell damned misguided emotion was driving her tie to him.

Not until hell froze over.

Nicole was still observing him. Waiting.

"Tell Jamie to go home," he muttered. "I don't want to see her."

Jamie wanted to scream in frustration. "What do you mean, he won't see me?" she demanded as she plopped into the visitor's chair in Nicole's office. She hadn't bothered to take off her coat and was stuffing her gloves into her pockets.

"Slade wasn't into elaborating. In fact, he was pretty angry about what has happened to him. But he was firm. Maybe he'll change his mind once he talks to the neurologist."

"And if he doesn't?"

"Then there's nothing I can do. I have to honor his wishes. He's a patient here at St. James. And even though he's my brother-in-law and I think he's making a helluva mistake, as a doctor, I have to do what he asks."

"Damn." Jamie leaned back in the chair and looked at the tiles in the ceiling. "He's just being stubborn . . . or thinks he's being noble . . . right now he needs all the support he can get."

Or maybe he really doesn't want to see you.

No, she wouldn't believe that. Not after the way he'd made love to her, after the way he'd kissed her at the car in the snow despite the fact that she told him she might marry Chuck.

"I agree about the support," Nicole said. She leaned back in her chair and nervously toyed with a pen. "But, unfortunately, he doesn't see it that way. Let's just give him some time to come to grips with his situation."

"I don't think it would help."

"It might."

Jamie was on her feet and it was all she could do not to rush out of the office, run up the stairs to the third floor and find a way to get through the locked doors of ICU. "I don't care what Slade says, I want to see him, I *need* to see him, and whether he admits it or not, he needs me. Right now."

Nicole looked bone-weary. And in no mood to take on an argument. "I told him I thought it was a mistake, but he was adamant. I don't know what went on between the two of you and I really don't need to know. It's your business. But, for the time being, I think, you should give it a rest. After he's talked with the neurologist and been moved to his own room and had some time to think things over, then he might change his mind, but for now, it would be best to let him have his way. He's going through a lot."

"He needs family around him. Friends.

People who care."

"Meaning you."

"Yes!" She clenched her fists at the impossibility of the situation.

"That may be so," Nicole said as her pager beeped. "But, speaking as a professional, I really do think the best way to do that is to leave him be. Let him work things out." She leaned across the desk where a cup of coffee sat untouched, papers were piled in an overflowing In basket and a bifold picture frame displayed glossy prints of her twins. "Now, speaking as a woman, one who herself couldn't resist the charms of a McCafferty brother, let me give you some advice. Let Slade come to you. That's the only way it'll work between you."

Jamie wanted to argue, to pull out all the ammunition in her arsenal to convince Nicole that she should see him, but the honesty in the doctor's face, the concern in the curve of her mouth, and the clearness of her eyes convinced Jamie to let it go.

"I really have to go," Nicole said, standing as her pager bleated again. "But I'll be in touch. I promise." Rounding the desk, she gave Jamie a hug, as if they were sisters, part of a family.

Which was ludicrous.

Slade had rejected her once before.

And he was doing it again.

Whatever his reasons, he was letting her know that he didn't want Jamie Parsons a part of his life. If she had any brains at all, she'd sell her grandmother's house to the first person who was interested, wrap up the title transfer of the Flying M, turn on her high heels and head out of town, to Seattle, or to San Francisco, or even to L.A. and find herself another job. One thousands of miles away from Slade McCafferty, the one man guaranteed to break her heart over and over again.

Kurt sat in his motel room, a beer on the scarred wooden table, the television flickering at the foot of his too soft bed. Barely a week before Christmas and he was stuck in Montana trying to figure out why Randi McCafferty was holding out on him and her family. He glanced at the TV screen. The local news had moved away from the recent McCafferty family tragedy that had taken the lives of two horses and had landed one of the brothers in the hospital. Now the anchorwoman was talking about the Christmas season.

Well, fa-la-la-la-la-the damned-la. The holidays were always a pain . . . or had been in the past few years. He didn't want to go there. Didn't want to think of the time before. Right now he had to concentrate on the McCaffertys.

It had been three days since the stables had burned, and the preliminary reports were in, reports that Kelly Dillinger, through her connections with the sheriff's department, had been able to peruse.

As was suspected, the fire had been intentionally set. Arson. Probably attempted murder. The press had had a field day with that turn of events and still the rumors around town persisted that one of the brothers was behind all the trouble at the Flying M.

Worse yet, the insurance company, Mountain Fire and Casualty, was balking at paying the claim because of the suspected arson. A claims adjuster had already been out and a private investigator, a guy Kurt knew, had been hired by the insurance company. It was Mountain Fire and Casualty's position that the fire could have been set by anyone on the ranch, especially the owners.

All in all, it was a helluva mess.

And it had all started with Randi McCafferty and her baby. Why was she so reticent to name the kid's father? It had crossed his mind that she didn't know the paternity of her own child, but he'd checked her out through friends, co-workers, landlords — everyone she'd come into contact with in Seattle. Though she'd been in several relationships over the past ten years, she wasn't into the bar scene, nor did it seem that she was likely to participate in one-night stands. He'd bet a year's retainer that she knew damned well who the little boy's dad was.

Amnesia, *shamn*esia.

She remembered.

She just wasn't talking.

He thought before that she might open up to him, had seen the hesitation in those brown eyes of hers. But she'd held back. Why? Didn't she trust him? What did she think would happen?

He flipped through the photographs he'd taken, snapshots of the original car accident and the ranch and the charred remains of the stables. There were other pictures, as well — photos of the men with whom she'd been involved. Kurt stacked them in a pile and studied each one.

Brodie Clanton, about five-ten, with a physique honed at a private gym, was a lawyer and connected to big money in Seattle. His grandfather had been a judge. Brodie, with dark hair, an aquiline nose, a

Ferrari he only used on weekends, and multiple degrees from Stanford, had dated Randi last year. Rich, smart, running in the correct social circles, Brodie wouldn't want the taint of any kind of scandal. He had his own political aspirations.

In Kurt's opinion, Clanton was about as warm as the Northern Pacific. Potential Dad Number One.

Randi had also kept company with Sam Donahue, a big, blond, tough-as-nails cowpoke who was a part of the rodeo circuit. Rough and tumble in denim and leather, Donahue was the diametric opposite of Brooks Brothers' dressed Clanton. Number Two.

The third man Randi had been romantically linked to and, in Striker's opinion, Potential Dad Number Three, was Joe Paterno, a photojournalist who did freelance work for the *Clarion* and who had probably done the headshot of Randi in Striker's file. It was a great picture of Randi looking over a bare shoulder, her mahogany curls wild, her eyebrows arched, her brown eyes shining with mischief, as if she couldn't believe her own vampy pose. With cheekbones a runway model would kill for and a playful intelligence that had been captured on camera, Randi McCafferty was too damned sexy for her own good.

Paterno was an intellectual, who flew all over the world to take pictures of newsworthy incidents. Kurt had seen his work, and it was impressive. Paterno had an eye for the dramatic, the tragic and the humorous. In Striker's estimation, Paterno was the only one of those men who'd dated Randi who was good enough for her.

That thought surprised him. He'd better keep his feelings for the hot-headed Mc-Cafferty sister back where they belonged — at a level of suspicion and distrust unmixed with other, warmer emotions.

So, he wondered, tipping his bottle of Coors, had one of the men she'd been linked to held a grudge against her and the baby? Did any of these guys know about the kid? Maybe Kurt was barking up the wrong tree altogether. Maybe there was another reason someone was trying to scare Randi off. The housemaid, Juanita, had mentioned that Randi had been working on a book. Randi, under questioning, wasn't sure. Now what the hell was that all about? Where was it?

He made a couple of mental notes. Nicole had seen someone coming out of Randi's hospital room, someone dressed as a doctor, right before she'd stopped breathing, and they'd determined that whoever it had been — man or woman — it wasn't anyone on the hospital staff. So the would-be killer was an imposter; that wasn't a surprise.

As for the maroon paint on Randi's vehicle, potential evidence of her being run off the road, there had been no leads. Kurt had nearly exhausted his list of automobile repair companies. Either the vehicle had been driven out of state and repaired, hadn't been fixed or someone in a local auto body shop was lying.

Back to the kid's daddy.

If Randi was being reticent about the name of Joshua's father, there were other ways to narrow the field. The baby had been in the hospital, his blood typed. Now it was just a matter of determining if Clanton, Donahue or Paterno could have been the sperm donor.

If not, he'd be back at square one.

As for that damned phantom book, Striker would just have to keep looking.

He slid the photographs back into the file, pausing for one last glimpse of Randi. Man, she was sexy . . . probably too sexy for her own damned good.

"So, all in all, you were lucky." Dr. Nimmo peered at Slade through wire-rimmed glasses. A short man in a too long lab coat and loosened tie, he'd finished examining Slade and had talked in medical terms about tests, X rays, MRIs — all of which Slade had endured in the past two days.

"Funny, but I don't feel particularly lucky."

"I suppose not, but it could have been so much worse. You have a cracked vertebra, L-3 or lumbar three, and there was some pressure on your spinal cord, but the cord's intact."

"No damage?"

"Nothing serious to the cord. You'll be fine and soon. As I said, lucky."

"So I'll walk again?"

"Yes."

A two-ton weight lifted from Slade's shoulders. "When?"

"I can't say. It may take some time, but, unless something unforeseen happens, you should be on your feet again. You might need some physical therapy, but no surgery . . . now we just have to wait."

"When can I go home?"

"We'll see," Nimmo said, marking Slade's chart. "I'll have a better idea in a day or two." He exited the room with a clipped-heel march and Slade stared out the window to the parking lot. The snow had stopped falling, but all the cars in the lot were covered with a blanket of white, the shrubbery hidden, the asphalt visible in black patches where the heat from exhaust and tread from tires had worn through the icy mantle.

He glanced at the clock and thought he'd go out of his mind. His family had visited and Nicole, it seemed, at least for the first thirty-six hours, had kept a vigil. A couple of times she'd mentioned Jamie, but Slade had refused to be pulled into that conversation. He thought of her nearly every waking moment, remembering what she'd said while he was drifting in and out of unconsciousness, recalling in vivid detail their lovemaking in the barns, fields and back seat of his Chevy that hot summer so many years ago. Then there was their recent encounter in the hayloft a few days ago. While the snow had drifted down and some jerk had trip-wired the door, they'd made love the way it was supposed to be. Hot, passionate . . . Her image came to mind and for the first time in days he felt a twitch . . . the hint of feeling . . . below his waist.

Was it possible? He tried to move his legs and failed, so he closed his eyes, conjured up Jamie's face — white skin softly dusted with freckles across the bridge of her straight nose. Lips that were full and stretched across the sexiest set of teeth he'd ever seen. And her eyes . . . an interesting shade of hazel that had darkened with desire when they'd been in the hayloft. Her kiss had sizzled, her hands, skimming down his body, touching and exploring, had caused his skin to fire and her tongue, wet, slick, agile . . .

There it was again.

The sensation in his crotch was familiar. And oh, so welcome. He felt himself thicken for a second . . . just enough time to give him a sliver of hope.

"I'm sorry, Jamie, but Slade doesn't want to see you." Nicole's voice was firm, but she couldn't hide the edge of concern in her words. "He's been moved to a private room, but he's been very insistent."

"Why?" Jamie asked, her heart breaking.

"I don't know."

"Is he walking?"

"He's trying."

"But he has feeling in his legs?"

"Yes. Look, technically I can't give out this kind of information. You know that."

"Of course I do. I'm a lawyer. I've had the classes, but I need to know, damn it."

"Please . . . just be patient."

"I'll try," Jamie lied, but the minute she

hung up the phone, she grabbed her jacket and threw it over her jeans and sweater. She pulled on her boots and took the time to pet Lazarus and feed Caesar, then climbed into her car. She tore out of her grandmother's driveway and caught a glimpse of the For Sale sign at the end of the lane. Snow clung to the post supporting the sign, and her grandmother's advice to never sell the place echoed through her mind.

She felt a moment's regret and considered staying in Grand Hope. She was at home here. The house was paid for. She could start her own firm, hang up her shingle, maybe find another attorney who wanted a partner and someone to share expenses. She had a home complete with cat, horse and vintage car. What more could she want?

The answer was blindingly simple. She wanted Slade. And she'd always gone after what she wanted with a vengeance. She snapped on the radio.

Jamie turned toward town. Toward the hospital. Toward Slade McCafferty.

Slade fell onto the bed. Drenched in sweat from the effort of trying to force his damned legs to move as the physical therapist had urged him along a contraption that looked like parallel bars straight out of the Olympics from hell, he'd trudged slowly, the length of the contraption looking a hundred miles long rather than a mere eight or ten feet.

From physical therapy he'd been wheeled back to his room and now the damned wheelchair was parked in a corner, wedged between a tiny closet and the bed, mocking him for his dismal effort today.

It's going to take time, he'd been warned by his doctors and Thorne who had handed him a burned piece of metal . . . the pocket watch his father had given him. It sat on the rolling stand next to a box of tissue and a water pitcher. Slade reached for the time-piece and remembered his father's insistence that it was time for his youngest son to settle down, to get married, to start a family. Well, he'd tried that. And failed. Twice.

Pain started rolling down his legs and he winced, but was grateful for the sensation, for the misery. With pain came hope that he would be whole again.

He'd just closed his eyes when he heard someone enter. *Don't bother me,* he thought, then got a whiff of perfume . . . a scent he recognized. His heart jumped into over-drive.

"Slade?"

"I thought I told everyone I didn't want to see you." He didn't open his eyes. Didn't think he could bear the sight of Jamie.

"But I thought it was a crock. So I sneaked past security. It wasn't that tough. You know the nurses, doctors and aides, they have other patients to deal with. I know sometimes you think you're the center of the universe, but not everyone feels the same."

He almost laughed. Almost.

"I think you said you didn't want to see me because it's some kind of macho thing with you, because of the accident. Face it, McCafferty, you're in denial."

"So now you're a shrink."

She hesitated. Taking a quick breath, she said slowly, "Just someone who cares."

Oh, God, did he dare believe her? No way. She was doing the noble thing, being the doting woman, playing a part. He remembered what she'd said to him, the vehemence of her words.

"Go away."

"No."

"I'll call the nurse."

"Then I'll be back."

"I could have you arrested."

"Go ahead."

He couldn't stop himself. His eyes flew open, and he found himself staring into the most beautiful face he'd ever seen. Her hair was pinned haphazardly to the top of her head, some of the strands falling in disarray, she wasn't wearing any makeup that he could discern and yet she was drop-dead gorgeous.

"I thought you were marrying Chuck."

"Nope. Never. He knew it. I knew it."

"But you told me . . ."

"You were being a jerk, if I recall." She grabbed his hand. "We've been through this once before — a long time ago when you left me and I never had the chance to say what I felt. This time I'm not going to blow it, okay? This time I want you to understand. I love you. It's that simple. It might not make any sense — in fact, it might not be the smartest emotion I've ever embraced, but it's true. I love you. And it doesn't matter that you're injured. It doesn't even matter if you don't completely heal. I love you."

His throat felt thick. He wanted to argue with her, to tell her that she was wrong, but he saw the conviction in her gaze, felt her take his hand and squeeze, noticed that tears had formed in the corners of her eyes.

"I'm . . . I'm really sorry about the baby." He forced the words out.

"Me, too . . . both of them . . ." A tear slid down her face. "Why didn't you tell me?"

she asked.

"Why didn't *you* tell *me?*" He saw her pain, understood.

"Two children . . . Oh, God, Slade, you've lost two. I wish there was something I could say or something I could do . . ."

His jaw was so tight it ached. How many times had he looked at Thorne's stepdaughters or little J.R. and thought of the children he'd never met? And now . . . He cleared his throat, fought his own tears. "Life goes on."

"And there will be more."

"Maybe not." He found that hard to believe, because even just looking at her he felt a twitch, a heating in his groin. . . . Oh, yeah, staring at her he began to grow hard. He smiled despite the pain. "There's no guarantee that this isn't permanent," he said.

"I know."

"You could —"

She pressed a finger to his lips. "There's no guarantees in life period, Slade. We both know that. We've both suffered enough. But . . . and this is a big point, I want to spend the rest of my life facing those challenges with you."

She withdrew her hand and he stared up at her. "That sounds damned close to a proposal."

One side of her mouth lifted. "See . . . you're smarter than you look."

"What about your job?"

"I've already quit. What about yours?"

"That's kinda up in the air right now. I had thought about . . ." His voice drifted away again. He didn't want to think about what he might not be able to do.

"What?"

He let his gaze slide away.

"What, damn it?"

"Before this, I'd thought . . . well, I figured I might take my share of the proceeds from the ranch and start a business. Tours. White-water cruises. Hiking expeditions. Skiing vacations, maybe even start my own dude ranch, advertise to city people . . . that sort of thing. But that was before the accident."

"So everything's changed?"

"Yes," he said. "Until I walk again."

"Well, you're right. Things have changed. But whether you walk again or not — and the way I hear it, you will — you could still run the business, maybe not be the guide per se, but you could still organize the trips, go out and explore. And you'd have me. I could help . . . well, in between making a fortune as the primary partner in the law firm of Jamie Parsons, Attorney-at-Law."

"It would never work."

"You're right. With that attitude." She leaned over the bed rail. "Come on, Slade. Don't give up. We lost each other once. Let's not do it again. What do you say?"

Nearly ripping out his IV, he wrapped a hand around the back of her head and pulled her face to his. His lips found hers and it felt so right, so natural. The hospital room seemed to fade away, and in his mind's eye, he saw the future with Jamie as his wife and kids surrounding them. They were all running through a field of tall grass, one little girl on Slade's shoulders, Jamie holding the hands of two older boys. Their kids. The sun was bright, reflecting on the waters of a clear creek that ran through the field. . . .

"What do I say?" he repeated into her open mouth, his nose touching hers. "Haven't I been saying it ever since I saw you again. I love you. I always have. You're the one who wouldn't listen. I've spent every waking hour of the past few weeks trying to convince you that we should start over, because you're the one woman in the world for me. The one. Do you hear me, Jamie Parsons, Attorney-at-Law?"

She gave out a soft little moan as he

released her. "I hear you, cowboy. Loud and clear."

Slade's throat tightened, and he felt her tears falling against his face.

"All right, Counselor, you win. I'll marry you."

She laughed and wiped at her eyes. "How romantic."

"It will be," he promised, pulling her face to his again, heat racing through his veins. From the corner of his eye he caught a glimpse of the charred pocket watch. *Yeah, old man,* he thought, feeling as if his father could see him. *You were right. It is time for me to settle down. With this woman. Forever.*

EPILOGUE

The wedding was perfect. Half the town of Grand Hope had been packed into a tiny church near the old railway station and now the ranch house, bedecked with holly, candles, fir boughs and hundreds of tiny lights, was jam-packed. It was two weeks after Christmas but the ceremony, like the Christmas festivities at the Flying M, had been postponed until Slade had been released from the hospital.

Jamie had held her breath, half expecting another tragedy to befall the McCafferty clan, but in the three weeks since the fire at the stables, things had been quiet. And Slade was healing. Slowly, but surely.

Music played from speakers throughout the house and most of the guests wandered through the living room, dining room and kitchen as well as the back porch that had been draped with insulated tenting material and festooned with billowing lace and warmed by dozens of space heaters.

Matt, dressed in a black Western-cut suit, and Kelly, in a sparkling wedding dress, danced and kissed, laughing with the guests and, it seemed, paying particular attention to Kelly's parents.

Jamie had heard there had been bad feelings when Matt had started dating Kelly, as her mother, Eva, had once worked for John Randall and somehow gotten the shaft financially. Though no one was saying too much, Jamie had come to the conclusion that John Randall's heirs had made it up to the Dillingers. Even Karla, Kelly's sister, who, Kelly had insisted, had sworn off men, was dancing and drinking champagne and flirting with some of the unattached male guests. She'd streaked her hair a dozen shades of blond for the event and was an interesting, if unconventional maid of honor.

Randi, too, was mingling with the single men and dancing. To Jamie's amusement, Kurt Striker watched her every move. Was he acting as her bodyguard or a potential lover? The twins were having a ball. Dressed in matching red velvet dresses, white tights and black shoes, they tore through the guests, only to be picked up by this uncle or that and swept around the dance floor.

Even the baby, in a tiny tuxedo complete with bright red bow tie, little cummerbund and snap crotch, made an appearance. Jamie's heart filled . . . to be a part of this family was overwhelming. She'd watched as Thorne had toasted the couple, then cast his own wife a sexy smile.

But as she glanced outside, Jamie saw the stables, barely more than a patch of rubble, with a few remaining blackened posts visible. Throughout the service and reception, she'd noticed the ever-vigilant bodyguards and undercover police, half expecting another attack.

She heard movement behind her. "Care to dance?" Slade said from his wheelchair.

She grinned down at him. "With a scoundrel like you?"

The gleam in his eye was wicked. "A guy can hope."

"I would love to."

"Good." He pushed himself out of the chair and teetered a bit.

"Oh! I thought you were kidding!" He'd improved with the physical therapy, of course, could sometimes walk with a crutch, but this . . .

"Come on . . ." He winked at her. "You won't let me fall, will you?"

"Never."

He swept her into his arms and listed a bit, then when she gasped, grinned down at her. "Gotcha."

"You miserable . . ." His arms surrounded her. "You're right. You do have me, Slade McCafferty," she admitted, "and I'm here to tell you, you'll never get rid of me."

"Even if I try?"

"Especially then." She winked at him and thought of the nights they'd spent together since he'd been released from the hospital, the lovemaking, gentle at first, but intense as he'd healed.

They danced a few bars and then she saw the beads of perspiration dotting his brow. "Whoa . . . cowboy. I think you've had enough for one day. Besides, you've got to save your strength."

"Do I? What have you got in mind?"

"A special little dinner . . . just you and me . . . in bed." They'd converted the dining room in her grandmother's house to a living room and Slade had been staying with her. "I think we need to celebrate."

"Because Matt's no longer a bachelor."

"Hmm. That, too."

"And because you've agreed to marry me."

"Yes, that, and it was *you* who agreed to marry *me*. But there's something else."

315

"No one's ruined the wedding."

She helped him off the dance floor and they stood, propped against the staircase. "I guess that could be part of it."

"There's something else?"

"Oh, yeah." Her eyes twinkled. "I have a surprise for you."

"What is it?"

"Something special. But it won't be delivered until late next summer."

"Can I wait that long?"

"You'd better." She saw a spark of understanding in his eyes. "Because then, cowboy, you're gonna be a daddy."

She saw the emotion in his eyes, the way his throat worked. "Jamie . . . I . . . You don't know what this means to me. I've lost two children already. Nothing . . . nothing could make me happier!" Without another word, he kissed her hard. As if he would never let her go.

"Let's elope," he finally whispered into her ear, and she grinned widely. "Tonight."

"I . . . I . . . but . . ."

"Come on, Counselor, where's your sense of adventure?"

"It's with you," she said.

"Then let's go. Time's awastin', and there's been enough of that already." He took her hand and, walking unsteadily, wended his way through the crowd, only stopping long enough to whisper something to his sister. "Don't tell a soul until tomorrow," he warned, then pressed a kiss to his nephew's head.

"For the record, I think you're crazy," Randi said.

"You always have."

With a laugh, Slade guided Jamie to the front door.

Outside, snow was falling, the January wind bitter and cold.

For the first time in her life, Jamie didn't notice. Her heart was warm and she glowed from the inside out. In a few short hours, she'd become Mrs. Slade McCafferty.

The adventure was just about to begin.

ABOUT THE AUTHOR

Lisa Jackson is the bestselling author of over sixty books, ranging from historical romances to romantic suspense to thrillers. Her work has appeared on the *New York Times, USA TODAY* and *Publishers Weekly* bestseller lists. Look for more classic Lisa Jackson stories coming soon from HQN.

The employees of Thorndike Press hope you have enjoyed this Large Print book. All our Thorndike and Wheeler Large Print titles are designed for easy reading, and all our books are made to last. Other Thorndike Press Large Print books are available at your library, through selected bookstores, or directly from us.

For information about titles, please call:
(800) 223-1244

or visit our Web site at:
www.gale.com/thorndike
www.gale.com/wheeler

To share your comments, please write:
Publisher
Thorndike Press
295 Kennedy Memorial Drive
Waterville, ME 04901